Where Spirits Walk

The Fragrance of Nard

by F J Barrett

F J Barrett

Published by
Doctor's Dreams Publishing
Biloxi, MS USA

Prepared in the United States of America

ISBN: 978-1-942181-60-6

Where Spirits Walk

The Fragrance of Nard

Table of Contents

Chapter 1

"So, your name is Thomas J. Baker?" Jerry Angelo asked, scanning the job application.

Tom nodded, and then added, "Yes, sir," when the manager looked up.

Angelo had a round, almost cherubic face, but the impression of warmth was undercut by his hard eyes and thin lips—lips that curled into a sardonic grin, as if he knew something about you that you didn't. His graying hair contrasted with his dark eyes and thick black eyebrows. He wore a snug brown Polo shirt, khaki trousers, and black work shoes. One foot was propped casually on the desk.

Leaning back, Angelo asked, "What's the J stand for?"

"Jared. But I just go by Tom."

"Any relation to the Bakers in Lewistown?" Angelo raised an eyebrow.

Tom shook his head. "We think they might be distant cousins, but we've never confirmed it."

"I see," Angelo said, pursing his lips like it was a mark against him. He flipped through the application, scanning for job-relevant details.

"You live in town and worked a few odd jobs since graduating high school three years ago," he said. "Not for long, though." He looked up, squinting. "What happened? Trouble with coworkers or the boss?"

Tom shifted in his seat. "No, sir. I worked those jobs during summer breaks between college semesters."

Angelo flipped to the education section and grunted. "Two years at State. What are you studying?"

Tom brightened. "Anthropology."

Angelo kept reading, unimpressed. "So, what's anthropology? Study of bugs or something?"

Tom chuckled.

Angelo looked up, irritated. "What's funny? Did I say something amusing?"

Tom straightened. "No, sir. It's just… anthropology studies cultures and lost civilizations. I thought it was funny—comparing bugs to people."

Angelo studied him for a moment, frowning like he'd been insulted. "Don't assume I'm dumb just because I didn't go to college. Got it?"

"Yes, sir," Tom said, shrinking back.

Angelo tossed the application on the desk, grabbed his half-finished, unlit cigar from the ashtray, and stood. He waved Tom to follow.

Tom trailed him out of the office, past the customer counter, to a door at the end of the counter. Angelo opened it and gestured inside.

Tom was stunned. The room was a fully furnished studio apartment. He'd visited U-Lock'em Storage plenty of times, but never knew this existed.

"Okay, Einstein," Angelo said, pointing with his cigar. "You've got the job—on probation. Make it through a week, and hold up to its demands, it's yours for the summer."

Tom nodded enthusiastically, adding a "Yes, sir" to show his appreciation. Still, he found it odd that Angelo had said "hold up to its demands"—how demanding could managing a self-storage facility really be?

"Since it's just you and me on payroll, you're the assistant manager," Angelo continued. "And in case you haven't figured it out…I'm the manager," he added with a smirk. He gestured toward the studio apartment. "You'll watch the facility nights and weekends. Weekdays, you're free to go home." He waited for Tom's nod before continuing. "You'll live here during your shifts. Food, toiletries, and whatever else you need—that's on you."

Tom nodded again, eager to begin. Angelo led him out of the apartment and toward a thick metal door near the customer counter—solid and imposing, like the entrance to a vault. He unlocked it with a key from his belt and motioned Tom through.

Crossing the threshold, Tom stood stunned again. As Angelo locked the door behind them, Tom stared down a wide corridor—at least ten feet across—lined with storage units on either side. He'd seen the outdoor units before, but never the indoor facility. The echo of the ventilation system hinted at the sheer size of the place. It felt enormous, like stepping into the belly of a mechanical beast.

"What's the matter, Einstein?" Angelo sneered. "Never been inside?"

Tom shut his gaping mouth and shook his head. “How big is it?”

Angelo chuckled. “You’re getting the grand tour. I want you to know this place inside and out.”

He pointed down the aisle with his cigar. “This is one of five just like it. Each has twenty garage-sized units, end to end. Exit doors at one end—locked with a code. Yours, mine, and the renter’s.” Tom spotted one of the exit doors with a small window at the far end. “Four more aisles cross left to right. Each of those has sixteen units, with exits at one end only. Total units? You’re the college boy—do the math.”

They turned into the first intersecting aisle. Tom saw the exit door to his left, and to the right, the corridor stretched deep into shadow. No exit door at that end, but he could make out the outline of a roll-up unit door in the dim light.

Angelo led him silently to the far exit door of the main aisle. As they walked, Tom absorbed the scale of the facility—it felt as vast as a starship. Every unit was metal-white, with roll-up garage-style doors reaching ten feet high. Overhead, pipes ran like arteries, sprinkler heads jutting downward. Above those, metal ventilation shafts hummed, working to maintain a steady temperature.

To Tom, it felt less like a building and more like a living machine.

Tom asked, “I noticed all the units are only so tall, with no ceilings. Doesn’t that pose a security problem?”

Angelo shook his head. “Each unit has a thick wire mesh overhead.” He pointed above them, where the mesh stretched across the aisle between units. Above it, pipes ran like veins. “It has to be mesh instead of solid metal so the air conditioning can circulate properly.”

"I see," Tom said, genuinely impressed.

Angelo led him to the nearest intersecting aisle near the far exit. Like the one by the office, this aisle also had an exit door. They turned down the corridor, passing the remaining four main aisles. To Tom, each looked identical—rows of metal-white units framed by overhead pipes. As they moved deeper into the facility, lights flicked on and off automatically.

"The lights are motion-sensored," Angelo explained. "They stay on for thirty seconds. If there's no movement, they shut off to save power."

Tom nodded. "Kind of gloomy back here."

"Not many people rent these far units," Angelo said. "They're bigger and cost more. Less traffic makes it feel quiet. Plus, there's only one exit door with a window at this end."

Tom glanced up and noticed the roof sloped higher here, and the air felt slightly cooler.

They walked the full length of the building, down each aisle, as Angelo explained the layout of unit numbers and emergency routes. He showed Tom how to monitor the sprinkler and A/C systems, where to find dollies and maintenance equipment, and emphasized keeping them accessible for customers.

Eventually, they stepped outside, where Tom was introduced to the outdoor units and keypad-operated security gates. As they passed the dumpster at the far corner of the property, Tom noticed a large hole in the ten-foot slatted fence—big enough for someone to crawl through.

He pointed it out. "What about that?"

Angelo shrugged. "Been there as long as I can remember," he said, brushing it off.

Back in the office, Angelo turned to Tom. "Any questions?"

Tom shook his head. Everything seemed straightforward enough.

"Okay," Angelo said. "Today's Monday. I want you here all day. I'll coach you on everything you need to do. Then, you'll stay the nights. Nights, you're on your own—call me if anything comes up. By the weekend, you should be able to handle things solo."

Tom nodded.

Angelo leaned forward. "This place is over five miles from town. Isolated. It gets dark and spooky out here at night. No business is conducted after hours, but some renters have 24/7 access. You might see one or two folks early evening, but after that—no one should be here. Especially late. If something feels off, don't take chances. Call me. Or the police. Got it?"

"Yes, sir," Tom said. He hesitated. "Earlier, you said 'if I am able to handle its demands.' What did you mean by that?"

Angelo leaned back, propping his foot on the desk. He was quiet for a moment, as if weighing his words. Then he held up a hand, fingers spread.

"I've had five assistant managers since this place opened six months ago. First guy lasted two months. The rest? Barely a month each. They all quit. Said they couldn't handle the isolation—being alone here at night."

Tom scoffed. "What, were they afraid of the dark?"

Angelo leaned in, his tone serious. "I don't know. But when night falls here, it falls hard. After 9 pm, nothing drives past. We're surrounded by forest on three sides. That two-lane road out front? That's your only link to civilization. You're alone. No one hears you in the night."

He picked up the office phone. "This is your lifeline in an emergency." He set it down again. "Some people just can't take the silence. The solitude. Like my former assistants."

Tom searched for words. "But nothing happened to them, right? No wild animals, no ghosts, no… demons?"

Angelo shrugged. "Not that I know of. They never gave details. Just called me later and said they quit. Wouldn't even come back to collect their things."

Tom raised an eyebrow. A haunted storage facility? He'd studied enough anthropology to know that ghost stories often served as moral warnings—tools to keep people in line. But this place was new. It had no haunted history.

He gave Angelo a crooked grin. "You ever stay the night to see what they were so afraid of?"

"Sure," Angelo said casually. "I've experienced things I couldn't explain. Mostly, I stayed holed up in the studio apartment. Didn't wander much."

A heavy silence settled between them.

"So, are you up to the challenge, Einstein?" Angelo finally asked.

Tom didn't care for the nickname, but he needed the job. "Yes, sir," he said.

Angelo smiled knowingly. "Good. Let's get you started."

Tom spent the rest of the day learning the ropes of managing the remote facility. It wasn't brain surgery, but he kept his opinions to himself, wary of provoking Angelo's disdain. The manager coached him through filling out lease agreements as customers wandered in, answering frequently asked questions, and processing monthly payments from regulars. He also walked Tom through basic maintenance—checking the network of pipes for leaks, monitoring the A/C thermostat, and inspecting the perimeter every few hours and at closing to ensure all doors were secure, trash was collected, and equipment returned to its proper place.

All in all, it seemed like a fairly easy job. Tom made careful notes, compiling a list of duties for both day and night shifts.

Angelo also introduced him to a few regular customers. One was a man in his mid-forties named Foster who rented an outdoor unit near the dumpster to store lawn service equipment.

"He's kind of a grouch," Angelo said. "Doesn't like to talk. Very defensive. I once pointed out an oil spill inside his unit—looked like it came from one of his mowers. He blew up, said it was there before he moved in. I let it go, but he's the only one who's ever rented that unit."

Later, Angelo showed Tom how to operate the outdoor surveillance cameras from the office. One feed showed an older Black couple unloading odds and ends from a unit.

"That's the Steagers," Angelo said. "Sweet people. They store items they sell online. That, my friend, is their livelihood. Doesn't look like they make much, judging by their car and inventory. Their rent's gone up twice since they started, but I haven't had the heart to tell them."

Tom glanced at him, surprised. Maybe beneath all that gruffness, Angelo had a soft spot.

"There's an indoor unit opening up soon," Angelo added. "I'm going to offer it to them at the same rate. I think the old man has a heart condition—he shouldn't be out in this heat."

Later that afternoon, as Tom sorted rental agreements, a loud banging rattled the metal door leading to the indoor units. His heart jumped. He cautiously approached, unlocked the door, and opened it.

A middle-aged man in coveralls stood on the other side, glaring at Tom with a look of pure consternation.

"Yes, sir," Tom said. "Can I help you with something?"

"You certainly can, Sonny!" the man growled, pointing toward the far side of the facility. "The exit gate's stuck halfway open. I can't get out."

Unsure what to do, Tom replied, "Okay. Just a minute." He left the man at the door and knocked on Angelo's office.

After hearing the complaint, Angelo checked the camera monitors. Sure enough, the exit gate on the opposite side of the building stood partially open.

"That happens from time to time," he murmured. He reached for a nearby control panel and pressed a button. On the monitor, they watched the gate close. Angelo then pressed another button, and the gate opened fully.

They stepped out of the office and found the man still waiting, arms crossed, irritation etched on his face.

"Sorry about that, Mr. Stevens," Angelo said. "It's a stubborn gate sometimes."

Stevens nodded curtly and turned away. "Well, maybe it's something that needs fixing."

Angelo smirked as the man huffed off. Back inside, he said, "Stevens is a regular. He's really not that bad. Big shot in town—doesn't like seeing machinery fail. Probably reminds him of the headaches in his own office."

At the end of the business day, Angelo handed Tom his final instruction. "Time to make your rounds."

Tom nodded and stepped out the front office door.

Outside the lobby door, Tom found the entrance gate fully closed and secured. He began his patrol, walking the full length of the outdoor units to ensure each door was properly shut and locked. Unoccupied units bore bright red locks—standard issue—and the office held the master key.

The outdoor units wrapped around three sides of the indoor facility, with the fourth side bordering the road. On the far end of the property sat the exit gate. It was a long walk from entrance to exit. Along the way, Tom picked up scattered trash and even pushed a child's abandoned scooter to the dumpster for disposal.

Tom noted the outdoor cameras mounted at strategic points near the roofline of the main building. They appeared to cover the entire facility. A few additional cameras were fixed to the outdoor units, aimed toward the central structure.

As he turned away from the dumpster, a sudden scurrying sound caught his attention. He stepped cautiously to the side and peered at the hole cut into the perimeter fence. With the sun already dipped behind the trees, the opening looked like a mouth into darkness. He listened for a moment longer, but no further sound followed.

Completing his circuit, he entered through the farthest door to the indoor facility and began patrolling each aisle. He retrieved bits of trash and returned unused dollies left behind by customers. As he moved through the dim corridors, motion sensors triggered the overhead lights—brief bursts of illumination that faded thirty seconds later, casting the space behind him into darkness once more.

Back in the front office, Angelo was waiting near the counter, briefcase at his feet, ready to head home.

"Well," he said, unlit cigar still pinched between two fingers, "think you can handle it until tomorrow, Einstein?"

Tom nodded. He was beginning to wonder if the cigar was just an extra finger.

Angelo gave him an appraising look, then picked up his briefcase. “Just remember—don’t hesitate to call if you have questions or concerns. If you see anything illegal, call the police. Don’t put yourself in danger.”

“Yes, sir,” Tom replied.

And with that, Angelo was out the door.

By 7:30 p.m., as darkness settled over the compound, Tom watched the last customer exit through the gate. Amber-colored security lights flickered on automatically, casting a dull glow across the outdoor units. He scanned the monitors carefully—no movement, no lingering vehicles. The premises were clear.

To cut costs, Angelo hadn’t installed indoor cameras, so Tom made another sweep through the facility. He walked each aisle, checked every exit door and unit, and confirmed everything was secure.

Back in the studio apartment, Tom prepared supper—a delicately microwaved TV dinner of enchiladas, rice, and beans. He left the apartment door slightly ajar to the office, just in case someone knocked, though technically the office was closed until morning.

Settling in, he switched on the television and reached for his tray. That’s when he heard it—a noise. Faint, indistinct, but enough to catch his attention.

Curious, Tom pushed the tray aside, muted the TV, and listened.

Silence. Only the low hum of the A/C filled the room.

After a minute, he shrugged it off—probably just the building settling or the ventilation system kicking in. He restarted the program and reached for his first bite.

Then he heard it again. This time, a distinct thump.

Tom switched off the TV, stood, and stepped to the apartment door. He peered out into the office—no one at the entrance. Perplexed, he scanned the room, hoping to find something that might explain the sound. Nothing. Just the steady hum of the air conditioning.

He hesitated to return to his dinner, waiting instead—almost willing the sound to return.

It did.

A knock. Faint. On the apartment wall.

Tom walked over and pressed his ear to the surface. It wasn't a single thump, but a rhythmic tapping—cadenced, deliberate, like someone trying to signal for help or get attention. The pitch of the knocks shifted, rising and falling, growing louder. A Doppler effect, he thought. The sound was moving closer.

He frowned. The other side of the wall led to the indoor storage units. The knocking was coming from inside. Stranger still, it seemed to pass fluidly from one unit to the next.

How could that be?

He kept his ear pressed to the wall, listening. Then, just as suddenly, the rapping reversed direction. The sound faded, growing distant, until it vanished altogether.

Tom stepped back, listening to the silence. As before, only the steady thrum of the A/C remained.

Just to be sure, he pressed his ear to the wall again.

Nothing.

He was about to pull away when a loud bang exploded against the wall—right where his ear had been.

Tom fell backward, heart racing, breath ragged. He crab-crawled away from the wall, eyes wide.

But as quickly as it had come, the banging was gone.

It had happened. He was certain of it.

Tom lay on the floor for a full minute, trying to calm his racing heart. Slowly, after regaining his composure, he stood and made his way to Angelo's office. He picked up the phone and dialed.

It rang three times.

"Hello."

"Mr. Angelo, this is Tom."

A pause. Then, "What's the matter, Einstein? It's been, what—three hours? You quitting already?"

"Uh, no… no," Tom stammered. "I just needed to call and say I think there might be an intruder on the premises."

Another pause. "Okay. Talk to me. What's going on?"

Tom described the rapping sounds, the movement along the wall, and the sudden bang that knocked him to the floor.

Angelo sighed. "So, you're calling me because you're spooked by knocking?"

Tom winced. It did sound childish—like he was afraid of the dark. "But it wasn't random," he insisted. "It sounded… intentional."

A long silence followed. Then Angelo said, "Look, kid. It's a big, hollow building. Mostly metal. Heats up during the day, cools down at night. Places like that make all kinds of noises—some you've never heard before. Did you check to see where it was coming from?"

"Well… no," Tom admitted, sheepishly. He felt like the Cowardly Lion.

"Check the monitors. Any suspicious activity outside? Any vehicles parked where they shouldn't be?"

Tom scanned each screen. The compound was quiet. "No. Everything looks normal."

"Okay," Angelo said. "We're halfway there. Unless someone climbed a ten-foot fence and broke into a locked building, it's probably just the facility settling. I'll call the police and have them send a patrol car to drive by the blind side—the street-facing wall you can't see on the monitors."

Tom nodded, even though Angelo couldn't see him.

"Meanwhile," Angelo continued, "I need you to put on your big-boy pants and walk the inside storage area. Check every door. Make sure they're locked. That's what I hired you for, right?"

Tom gulped. "Yeah… I guess I can do that."

"You guess?" Angelo snapped.

Tom swallowed hard. "Yes. I can do it."

"That's a good boy," Angelo said, dripping sarcasm. "If it'll make you feel better, there's a can of mace in the bottom drawer of my desk. Take it with you. Call me back when you've made your rounds."

Then he hung up.

Tom replaced the receiver and opened the bottom drawer. No mace. He sifted through piles of paperwork and found a cigar box. Assuming the mace might be inside, he opened it—and froze.

A revolver.

Angelo hadn't mentioned a gun. Maybe he didn't want Tom to know it was there. Gingerly, Tom lifted it. Fully loaded. Feeling like he'd crossed some invisible line, he returned the weapon to the box and closed the lid.

He checked the bottom drawer on the opposite side of the desk and found the can of mace in plain view. He grabbed it, along with a flashlight, and retrieved the keys to the storage area from the wall hook.

Before heading out, he glanced at the monitors. A police cruiser was parked at the entrance gate. An officer stepped out, flashlight in hand, and began walking the perimeter along the street-facing side. Within seconds, he was out of view.

Now it was Tom's turn.

He approached the door to the indoor facility and pressed his ear against the cold metal, listening for any sound—knocking, movement, anything.

Silence.

With mace at the ready, he unlocked the door and opened it a crack. Darkness spilled through. The office lights illuminated only a few feet beyond the threshold. Beyond that—nothing.

He knew the automatic lights wouldn't activate until he stepped inside.

Swallowing his fear, he crossed the threshold. Instantly, the lights flared on, stretching down the aisle to the far exit. The corridor glowed with sterile brightness. Nothing seemed out of place.

Flashlight and mace in hand, Tom began his patrol. Eight doors to check. Four in this aisle alone.

At the first intersection, he glanced left. The nearest door was just ten steps away. He swept his flashlight to the right, but the beam barely pierced the gloom. Peering over his shoulder, he stepped to the exit door and rattled the knob. Locked.

He moved quickly down the aisle, checking each exit. His footsteps echoed through the cavernous space, accompanied only by the constant low drone of the A/C. The farther he walked, the more it felt like descending into a black chasm. The office door was now more than 200 feet behind him.

All doors were locked.

Still, four more to go—along the far side of the facility.

Tom inhaled deeply and directed his flashlight down the final intersecting aisle. As he stepped forward, the lights behind him suddenly shut off, plunging him into darkness. Even his flashlight seemed weak, swallowed by the void.

He froze. Breath quickened. Pulse raced.

He swung the beam in all directions, but the shadows devoured it.

Closing his eyes, he took slow, steady breaths. He reasoned he'd passed the sensor range of the previous lights but hadn't yet reached the next set. Acting on that assumption, he stepped forward—tentatively, like walking a tightrope.

The lights flared on.

Relief flooded him.

He checked the exit door to his left. Locked. He repeated the process three more times. Each door secure.

Everything appeared normal. No signs of intrusion.

Feeling reassured, Tom strolled back toward the office, confidence returning. The noises earlier—just the groans and creaks of a metallic, mechanized structure. Artificial. Inanimate.

But just before reaching the office door, he heard it—a distinct rattle above.

He looked up.

The thick wire mesh ceiling vibrated, then settled.

He froze, pulse quickening again.

The sound had come from a distance. It wasn't repeated.

But it had happened.

Tom ran into the office and sealed the door behind him before anything else could happen.

Leaning against the counter, trying to calm his nerves, the intercom suddenly beeped—loud and sharp. He dropped to the floor instinctively, crouching behind the counter like it might shield him. A second beep followed.

Realization hit. Someone was at the entrance gate, calling through the intercom.

Tom slowly stood and checked the monitor. A police officer stood at the gate.

Embarrassed, he pressed the button. "Hello."

"Yes," came the reply. "This is Officer Jansen. Who am I speaking to?"

Tom nearly stuttered but caught himself. "Tom Baker. Assistant Manager."

A brief pause. Then, "I've completed a round at the front of the building. Everything looks secure. Are you okay? Do I need to come in?"

Tom hesitated, feeling foolish for the panic he'd stirred. "No. Everything's secure in here too. Thanks for checking."

The officer gave a wave, turned back to his cruiser, and drove off.

Tom was alone again.

He decided to finish his dinner quickly and go to bed.

Chapter 2

Tom spent a sleepless night in the apartment, jolting awake at every sound—the A/C cycling, the fridge humming, the ice machine dumping, the wall clock chiming. Each noise felt amplified, unnatural.

Then the phone in Angelo's office started ringing. Intermittently. Every time Tom rushed to answer, there was silence. No one on the line. It couldn't be Angelo—Tom had already called him after the police left to confirm everything was secure.

By 7:00 a.m., Tom was bleary-eyed and dragging. Angelo walked in wearing his usual dark brown polo and khakis. Tom figured his closet was full of them.

"What's the matter, Einstein?" Angelo smirked. "Up late studying your Archeology?"

Tom rubbed his eyes. "It's Anthropology, not Archeology."

Angelo shrugged, dropped his briefcase by the desk. "Whatever. You want to sit down and tell Papa all about it?"

Tom collapsed into the chair across from him and waved a tired hand. “The rapping sound must’ve gotten to me. I jumped at every noise. And just when I’d start to doze off, the phone would ring. No one there. It felt like someone was trying to keep me awake.”

Angelo frowned. “The phone rang all night? That’s a new one.”

Tom nodded, eyes half-closed. “It is? Why?”

Angelo leaned forward. “Just odd. That’s never happened to me. Or anyone else who worked here.”

He paused, then added, “You just need to get used to the routine—the noises, the isolation, sleeping in a strange place. It takes time.”

He gestured toward the door. “Go home. Get some rest. Be ready to take over again tonight at five.”

Tom nodded, too tired to argue, and lumbered out without a word.

At 5:30 that afternoon, Tom returned for his nightly shift, rested and in better spirits. He tiptoed around Angelo and restocked the studio apartment with food and snacks more to his liking. The night before, he’d been stuck with leftovers from past assistant managers—none of whom had returned to claim their goods.

Angelo eventually appeared at the open apartment door just as Tom was finishing up. “Come into my office when you’re set. I need to catch you up before I leave.” He vanished before Tom could respond.

Inside the office, Tom sat and waited while Angelo wrapped up a phone call, finalizing business details above Tom’s pay grade. He felt like a kid in the principal’s office, waiting to be scolded. As he stewed, he glanced at the monitors. Three showed customers rummaging through units packed with odds and ends—no rhyme, no reason. Tom wondered why people hoarded things they hardly used.

When Angelo finally hung up, he gathered the paperwork, filed some away, stacked others neatly, then turned to Tom. He leaned back, hands folded over his belly.

Before he could speak, Tom blurted out, "I'm sorry about last night. And I promise—"

Angelo raised a hand. "Forget it. Chalk it up to first-night jitters. Okay?"

Tom nodded.

Angelo gave a quick rundown of new and regular customers, plus tasks to finish before the week's end. Tom nodded again but didn't take notes this time.

Angelo eyed him. "So, you up for another night on the plantation, or are you planning to jump ship but don't have the balls to say so?"

The bluntness caught Tom off guard. "Well… I… no," was all he managed.

Angelo gestured. "Just noticed you didn't take notes. You're not as bright-eyed and bushy-tailed as yesterday."

Tom lowered his head.

"I don't beat around the bush anymore," Angelo said. "If you're planning to quit, let's get it over with so I can find someone else." He let that hang. "So, what's it gonna be, Einstein?"

Put on the spot, Tom squirmed. "No. I don't plan to quit anytime soon."

Angelo smirked, unconvinced, but nodded. "Good deal. Just remember—this is a big place. At night, when you're the only one here, you start to feel small. Vulnerable. I think people call it the 'fight or flight' instinct. We cower in the dark, listening for predators, hoping to survive."

Tom looked up, surprised by the insight.

Angelo chuckled. "Told you, Einstein—just because I didn't go to college doesn't mean I'm dumb."

He grabbed his briefcase and headed for the door. "Call me or the police if there's any trouble."

And he was gone before Tom could respond.

The evening began without incident. Tom moved through the outdoor facility with quiet purpose, picking up stray bits of trash, returning equipment to its proper place, and checking the locks on each storage unit. As he passed one of the units, a middle-aged woman was just finishing up, packing her car and closing the door behind her. He offered a polite nod, but she responded only with a scowl and a wary glance. Moments later, she drove past him on her way out of the complex.

Inside the building, Tom walked each aisle methodically. Every unit was closed and locked, and any trash or abandoned dollies had been cleared away. Satisfied, he returned to Angelo's office to check the monitors. Each screen showed a quiet, empty compound. But just as he turned to leave, something flickered in camera 3—the one aimed at the corner of the building near the dumpster.

He turned back quickly, but whatever had moved was already gone. The movement seemed to be in the direction of camera 4.

Curious, he watched camera 4, hoping to catch a glimpse of it again. Nothing. And nothing on the other cameras either. If something had been there, it was now hidden in the blind spot between cameras.

He continued watching, eyes scanning for movement. After several minutes, he began to wonder if he'd imagined it—until he noticed something strange near the dumpster.

The child's scooter.

It was leaning casually against the side of the dumpster, right next to the hole in the fence. But earlier, during his rounds, it hadn't been there. He was certain of it. He remembered placing the scooter on the opposite side of the dumpster the day before, ready for pick-up.

Just then, movement caught his eye again—this time in camera 4. A brief flicker, gone before he could focus. Someone—or something—was toying with him.

Determined to get answers, Tom opened Angelo's drawer and retrieved the can of mace. He grabbed the keys from the desk and stepped out through the lobby door, locking it behind him.

From where he stood, he could see the dumpster at the far end of the drive, its bulky frame silhouetted against the fading light. The outdoor units lined the drive to his left, like silent spectators watching the scene unfold.

The scooter was clearly visible now, leaning just as it had before. Tom glanced up at the sky. The sun was sinking behind the trees, casting long shadows across the pavement. He figured he had fifteen, maybe twenty minutes of daylight left.

With steady resolve, he began walking toward the dumpster.

But after only a few steps, he stopped.

At the corner of the building, a small head peeked out. A child—perhaps 10 years old—darted from the edge of the building to the back of the dumpster. The movement was so quick, he couldn't tell if it was a boy or a girl.

Tom stood frozen, unsure what to do.

Then, just as suddenly, the child reappeared, slipped through the hole in the fence, and vanished into the woods beyond.

"Hey… wait!" Tom called out, breaking into a run. He reached the fence and shouted again. "Wait! I'm not going to hurt you!"

But the child was gone.

From the darkness beyond the fence, he heard the heavy tramping of something large moving through the forest—branches snapping, low grunts echoing through the trees.

Tom backed away, heart pounding, suddenly fearful that a bear—or something worse—might be nearby.

After a minute, the forest fell silent.

Still stunned, and unsure what to make of what had just happened, he reached down, picked up the scooter, and tossed it into the dumpster.

Two hours had passed, and Tom still sat at Angelo's desk, idly tapping a pencil against the surface as he watched the TV monitors for any sign of movement. The facility had remained quiet since the fleeting glimpse of the child-like figure. But the image lingered in his mind, refusing to fade.

He kept asking himself: *Had I really seen something? A person… or something else? A ghost, maybe?* The questions circled endlessly. *Have I experienced ghostly activity last night and tonight? Is that even possible?*

His rational mind pushed back. *Ghosts don't exist. There's no such thing as hauntings—only haunted people. People use ghosts to explain what they don't understand.*

And yet, what unsettled him most was the realization that he wasn't above such notions. He had always considered himself a rational thinker, someone capable of explaining strange events through logic and science. But here he was, entertaining the idea of believing the unbelievable.

Maybe, he thought, *believing the unbelievable is instinctual—a part of human nature we never outgrow. Like the id, always lurking in the primitive corners of the mind, waiting to surface.*

Just then, his eyes drifted to the monitor for camera 3, and the pencil slipped from his fingers, clattering onto the desk.

In the dim glow of the sodium-vapor lights, the small scooter had reappeared—leaning against the dumpster exactly where he'd found it earlier. He stared at it, stunned, then slowly rose to his feet and began scanning the other monitors.

Two showed outdoor units with their doors wide open.

Then, on another screen near the exit, he watched in disbelief as a unit door rolled upward—no one in sight, no visible force behind it.

It was as if the facility itself were daring him to confront what his rational mind refused to accept.

His hand trembled as he reached for the drawer that held the mace. But he stopped.

Instead, he opened the drawer where the revolver was kept. It was still there, tucked beneath a stack of papers. He lifted the box, opened it, and checked the weapon. Still fully loaded.

He had never fired a gun before. Never found himself in a situation where he needed to. It felt foreign in his grasp—heavy, not just in weight, but in meaning. That heaviness seemed to amplify the seriousness of its purpose.

If someone was out there, they might be dangerous. And in that case, the weapon could be more than reassurance—it could be survival.

Tom stepped away from the desk, considering whether to call the police. Or at least Angelo. But the thought of being seen as jumpy, frightened by shadows, made him hesitate. He didn't want to be the guy who cried wolf every time the dark whispered.

So, he pushed the thought aside.

And with a deep breath and a surge of determination, he headed for the door.

As Tom exited the lobby door, he locked it behind him and slipped the keys into his pocket. The night air was still, and the complex lay bathed in the pale glow of security lights. But when he turned toward the dumpster, everything appeared normal. The storage units that had shown as open on the monitors were now closed.

He stood there for a moment, puzzled, then hurried back inside. Unlocking the door, he rushed to Angelo's office and peered at the monitors. His breath caught.

The doors were open again.

Without hesitation, he bolted back outside. But once more, the units stood closed, silent, undisturbed. "This is impossible," he muttered, stepping toward them. He checked each one. The locks were secure. He tucked the pistol into his belt to free his hands and tried lifting the doors. They didn't budge.

Tom stood in the middle of the drive, baffled. The complex was quiet, the lights steady, the air unmoving. There was no sign of tampering, no hint of mischief. Just stillness.

He continued toward the dumpster and found the scooter still inside, exactly where he had tossed it earlier. Scratching his head, he made his way to the unit near the exit gate—the one he'd seen opening on the monitor. It too was locked and secure.

Someone—or something—was playing with his mind. But was it a prankster? Or something else entirely?

With renewed resolve, he turned as if heading back inside, then quickly ducked into the shadows, slipping out of view of the cameras. He crouched low, unmoving, watching the complex as it slumbered beneath the muted light. From his vantage point, he could see in two directions. The dumpster was only thirty feet away, though the hole in the fence remained hidden from sight.

As five minutes passed, the only sound was the wind stirring the leaves beyond the compound. No movement. No flicker of light. No sound of footsteps or rolling doors. Everything remained perfectly still.

Ten minutes passed. Then another ten. He began to feel foolish, crouching in the dark like a child waiting for monsters. But he knew what he'd seen—the open doors, the scooter reappearing. It hadn't been his imagination.

Still, the compound remained silent. Inert.

Reluctantly, he gave up and returned to the office, reasoning that if it truly were a ghost, it would know he was hiding anyway.

Back inside, he glanced at the monitors once more.

The doors were open again.

He stared, mouth agape, then sank heavily into the chair across from Angelo's desk and buried his face in his hands.

The question of what to do weighed on him. He sat there for several minutes, trying to make sense of it all. In the end, he decided to push the anomaly aside and fix himself something to eat. After all, what he had seen with his own eyes—the closed and locked doors, the scooter in the dumpster—was what truly mattered. His senses confirmed reality. The monitors, on the other hand, could be manipulated. They could lie.

Television did it all the time. Dramas and sitcoms were crafted to mimic real life, but they weren't real. They were illusions. Carefully constructed.

Comforted by that thought, Tom returned to his apartment and tried to put the monitors, the storage doors, and the scooter out of his mind.

By bedtime, Tom felt more at ease. The tension from earlier had faded, and he found that Angelo had been right—the sounds of the apartment, once jarring and unfamiliar, had begun to blend into the background. The hum of the refrigerator, the soft click of the A/C, even the occasional chime of the wall clock—all of it now felt like part of the rhythm of the place. He drifted off more easily than the night before.

But at 2:00 a.m., the phone in Angelo's office rang, sharp and sudden, jolting him awake.

This time, he decided to ignore it. Whoever was calling could wait. Maybe they'd give up.

But the ringing continued. Relentless. Twenty rings passed, maybe more, before Tom finally gave in. He stumbled out of bed, shuffled into the office, and picked up the receiver.

"Hello, U-Lock'em Storage," he said, his voice thick with sleep.

There was silence. A beat. Then a click.

Tom muttered a curse and stared at the receiver in his hand. "Well, you're not going to keep me awake again tonight," he said aloud, more to himself than anyone else.

Instead of placing the receiver back on its cradle, he laid it on the desk and turned to leave. He was halfway back to the apartment, already imagining the comfort of his pillow, when the phone rang again.

He froze.

A chill crept up his spine.

He turned slowly, dread settling over him like a fog. Creeping back into the office, he flipped on the lights.

The phone was ringing.

And the receiver was back in its cradle.

Angelo found Tom seated in his usual chair across from the desk, his posture slack, eyes glazed and unfocused. He didn't glance up or acknowledge Angelo's presence as he stepped around him and set his briefcase down beside the desk.

Angelo sat, folded his hands on the desktop, and studied him for a moment. "You okay, kid?"

Tom's eyes slowly turned toward him, as if recognizing his boss for the first time. "Sure," he said weakly.

Angelo sighed. "You don't look it. Another rough night?"

Tom gave a faint nod, barely perceptible.

Angelo leaned in slightly. "Want to tell me about it?"

Tom spoke softly, his voice sluggish, as though searching for the right words. "The phone… it rang again. Over and over. No one there. And the monitors… they showed movement outside. But when I checked, no one was there."

Angelo pursed his lips and leaned back in his chair. "So, you're bothered because no one was there when they were supposed to be?"

Tom looked at him, confused. "No. I'm bothered because someone was there—and no one was there—at the same time."

Angelo shook his head. "That doesn't make sense, Einstein."

Tom blinked at the nickname, surprised. Angelo continued, "Something can't be there and not there at the same time. Right?"

Tom stood abruptly and began pacing in front of the desk. "I know that. The very idea violates the Law of Non-Contradiction."

Angelo remained quiet, letting him move through the moment. Eventually, Tom sat again, rubbing his eyes, and began recounting the events in detail. Angelo listened patiently, without interruption.

When Tom finished, Angelo asked, “So, when you went outside, were the doors open or closed?”

“Closed and locked,” Tom replied with a sigh.

“And the scooter—was it in or out of the dumpster?”

Tom looked up at the ceiling, wearied. “Inside the dumpster.”

Angelo took a deep breath. “Then what’s the problem?”

Tom pointed at the monitors, showing everything as normal, his voice rising. “The monitors. What about the monitors?”

Angelo shrugged. “What about them?”

“They showed the doors open. The scooter outside the dumpster. How do you explain that?”

“I don’t,” Angelo said simply. He paused, then leaned forward. “Maybe you only saw what you wanted to see on the monitors.”

Tom stood again, stunned. “Are you saying I imagined it?”

Angelo shrugged again. “What other explanation is there? When you checked, the doors were locked. The scooter was in the dumpster. That’s reality.”

Tom jabbed a finger toward the monitors. “Someone’s messing with me. Manipulating the feed. Maybe using a remote video loop or something.”

Angelo reached for the remote and held it out. “Okay, Einstein. It’s all yours. Trace the lines. Check the cameras. Look for antennas. Do your worst. Let me know if you find anything.”

Tom stared at the remote but didn’t take it. He knew Angelo was right. The system was clean.

"Well," he said, grasping for something solid, "what about the kid I saw? Running behind the dumpster and through the hole in the fence. That was real. I saw it with my own eyes."

Angelo looked away and muttered under his breath. "God, I've got to fix that damn hole before it drives me crazy."

He pushed back from the desk and stood. "Look, all I want to know is—are you quitting or staying?"

Tom hesitated, the weight of the question pressing down on him. Finally, he answered, defeated but resolute. "Staying."

Angelo nodded. "Good. Go home. Get some sleep. Be back at 5:30, rested and ready for the night.

Chapter 3

When Tom returned to work in the late afternoon, he threw himself into his duties, hoping to avoid any lingering tension with Angelo after the morning's exchange. Everything seemed routine—trash pickup, equipment checks, lock inspections—but he could feel Angelo's eyes on him. Whether from the opened office door or in passing, Tom sensed the quiet scrutiny. No words were exchanged until Angelo called him in just before leaving for the evening.

Tom entered the office quietly and took his usual seat, shoulders slightly hunched. Angelo didn't acknowledge him at first, continuing to sort papers and tidy the desk. Only when he was ready to leave did he speak.

"So, are you ready for the evening?" he asked, his tone clipped.

Tom nodded, saying nothing.

"Okay then," Angelo said. "As usual, call me if you need me. Call the police if it's an emergency." He stood, grabbed his briefcase, and paused at the door. "And a word of advice—don't go ghost hunting. If there's no intruder and the building's not falling in around your ears, let it go. You're paid to watch the property and assist customers. Not solve mysteries."

He waited until Tom responded with a quiet, "Yes sir," then left without another word.

As Tom moved through his closing duties, Angelo's advice echoed in his mind. Maybe that was how Angelo had lasted so long in the job—even during overnight shifts. He ignored the bumps in the night, resisted the urge to investigate, and kept his curiosity in check.

Ignorance must truly be bliss, Tom thought, wryly.

At the dumpster, he tossed in a few items and heard them land with a hollow thump. He hesitated, then glanced inside. It was empty except for the trash he'd just thrown in. He remembered the garbage had been collected earlier that day. Still, he looked around the sides of the dumpster, half-expecting the scooter to be leaning there again.

Nothing.

He exhaled, only then realizing he'd been holding his breath.

Back inside, he checked the monitors in Angelo's office. Three vehicles were parked beside outdoor units—one a pickup loaded with chairs and a table. On camera 4, a gold sedan sat near the far exit door of the indoor complex. After locking up and putting away the keys, he noticed the sedan had gone. Soon, the other vehicles exited the gate as well.

Tom stood at the glass door, watching the sun retreat behind the trees. The weight of isolation settled over him. Darkness crept across the pavement like spilled ink, filling cracks and climbing the walls. Then, with a soft hum, the sodium-vapor lights blinked on, casting their pale glow across the compound.

He felt a small measure of relief.

Turning away from the door, he headed to his studio apartment—quietly bracing himself for whatever the night might bring.

Munching his TV dinner—beef tips over rice—Tom reflected on the past two nights. Each had been distinct in tone and texture. The first was dominated by sound: faint rapping, knocking, the occasional pounding on the walls, and the rattle of the overhead wire mesh. Then came the familiar hums and clicks of the apartment, followed by the persistent ringing of the phone.

The second night had shifted into something more visual. The monitors. The unit doors opening. The reappearance of the scooter. The fleeting glimpse of the child-like figure. And again, the phone. But this time, even the phone had a visual twist—the receiver mysteriously returned to its cradle, as if by invisible hands.

As he rinsed his plate and set it aside, Tom considered that some of these experiences—the child specter, the scooter, the vibrating mesh—weren't just visual anomalies. They were physical. Tangible. Real.

He wondered what the third night might bring. Was it building toward something? A crescendo? A message?

The thought stirred something unexpected in him. Curiosity began to replace fear. But almost immediately, he caught himself. *Don't go ghost hunting,* Angelo had warned. *If there's no intruder and the building's not falling in around your ears, let it go. You're paid to watch the property and assist customers—not solve mysteries.*

Tom nodded to himself, as if reaffirming the boundary. To distract his mind, he flipped on the television and settled into the studio's lone recliner. The hours passed quickly, one program bleeding into the next. After the fourth show, he glanced at his watch—11:00 p.m. Already.

He felt a flicker of disappointment. Nothing had happened.

Switching to the local news, he caught a weather report: a strong storm system was expected to pass through in the early morning hours. He checked the time again. Nearly midnight.

Tom clicked off the set and began preparing for bed.

Before retiring, he shuffled into Angelo's office for one final check. The monitors showed a quiet compound—no vehicles, no scooter near the dumpster, all unit doors closed. He glanced at the phone. The receiver sat securely in its cradle.

As an added precaution, he unplugged the phone line from the wall jack and the base, coiled it, and carried it back to the apartment.

Settling under the covers, he listened to the distant rumble of thunder. The storm was approaching, slow and steady. The sound grew louder, rolling across the sky in waves.

But before long, sleep overtook him.

An explosion jolted Tom awake, shaking the bed beneath him. The blast was so deafening, his first thought was that the Aluminum Plant a few miles north had erupted into a massive fireball. He leapt from the bed, heart pounding, and stumbled to the television. Still groggy, he shook his head, trying to clear the fog from his mind.

He flipped through every local station—no reports of an explosion. Nothing.

Unconvinced, he threw open the apartment door and rushed to the lobby door. Pressing his face to the glass panel, he peered outside.

Roiling black clouds churned above the outdoor units, blending with the dark outline of trees. Their leaves fluttered wildly, limbs and trunks swaying like dancers caught in a frenzied, tribal ritual. Rain fell in sheets, hammering the metal roof with such force it sounded like a waterfall crashing overhead.

He listened carefully. No sirens. No distant alarms.

"Maybe it was just a dream," he whispered.

But then, a blinding flash of lightning split the sky, striking the forest just beyond the facility. The thunder followed instantly—an explosion that reverberated through the walls and floor. Tom fell backward, instinctively shielding himself. The shock rattled him to the core.

Panting, he struggled to catch his breath, as if he'd plunged into icy water.

Once steady, he stood and kept a cautious distance from the lobby door. Rain lashed against the glass in violent torrents. The door trembled in its metal frame, as though the wind itself were demanding entry.

The explosion he'd imagined at the Aluminum Plant must have been a close lightning strike. The thunder continued to roll, echoing across the sky as it faded into the distance.

Exhausted, Tom returned to his apartment and collapsed onto the bed. Another thunderclap shook the building—this time from the far side of the complex. The storm was moving on.

He drifted off again, lulled by the fading rumble.

But then—banging.

He sat up abruptly, swung his legs to the floor, and listened. The sound hadn't come from the storm. He was sure of it.

Everything was quiet now. Still. Yet he knew he'd heard it.

He sat at the edge of the bed, rubbing his eyes, trying to make sense of it. Then, suddenly, the banging returned—this time just outside his apartment door.

Cautiously, he stepped forward, opened the door a crack, and peered into the lobby. Darkness enveloped the space, broken only by the pale glow spilling in from the outdoor lights beyond the glass.

The banging resumed, louder now. He traced the sound to the door leading into the indoor facility.

His first instinct was to call Angelo. Or the police.

But he hesitated.

Not yet.

First, he needed to check the monitors.

Tom hurried to Angelo's office, heart pounding, and peered at the monitors. To his surprise, the gold sedan he'd seen earlier—parked outside the far exit door—had returned. It sat in the same spot, unmoving, as if it had never left.

As he stared, trying to make sense of it, the banging resumed—louder, more urgent. This time, he heard a voice behind it. Faint. A woman's voice.

Assuming it was a customer in distress, he rushed to the door and called out, "Who's there?"

There was no doubt someone was inside the complex. But who?

A muffled reply came through the metal. "Can you hear me? I need you to open up. Hurry!"

Tom dashed back to Angelo's office, retrieved the key, and unlocked the door. As it swung open, a young woman burst into the lobby like a shot—wild-eyed, soaked to the bone, and breathless.

Before Tom could speak, she turned and slammed the door shut behind her, the bang echoing through the empty space. Pressing her back against the metal frame, she slowly slid down to the tiled floor, her body trembling with relief.

Tom stood frozen, stunned by the suddenness of it all.

She sat slumped against the door, panting, her breath ragged and shallow. She looked to be about his age. Her blond hair hung in wet, stringy strands around her face. Her clothes—thin-strapped, striped top and faded jeans—clung to her skin, soaked through. Flat, open-toed sandals completed the picture. Despite her drenched, disheveled state, Tom found her face striking—blue eyes that shimmered even in the dim light, a small nose, delicate features, and ears that gave her an elfin quality. She reminded him of Tinker Bell, though her hair hung loose and limp rather than swept into a bun.

As her breathing slowed, she drew her knees to her chest, wrapped her arms around them, and lowered her forehead to rest on her arms, hiding her face.

Tom knelt beside her, his voice soft and steady. "It's okay. You're safe now."

She looked up, tears brimming in her eyes. "I'm sorry," she said, her voice breaking. "I got lost in there. I've been lost for too long. The lights went out, and I couldn't see anything. It was pitch black." She hiccupped through her sobs. "I finally found the door and just started pounding, hoping someone was there."

Tom reached out instinctively, then hesitated, unsure if she'd recoil from his touch. He let his hand fall and offered reassurance instead. "That's okay. I'm glad I was here to help."

He paused, then asked gently, "What's your name? How did you end up here in the middle of the night… in the storm?"

A few more sobs escaped her lips before she spoke again, the sound delicate and child-like. “My name’s Sandra. My things… they’re here.” She paused, then added, “The storm… the drenching water trapped me inside.”

Tom nodded quietly. He didn’t recall the lights going out during the storm, but it was possible they had while he slept. Everything in the office—the monitors, the television—had seemed to be working fine. Still, he let her speak without interruption.

“…that’s when I got lost.”

He stood and gently took her arm, helping her to her feet. “Let’s get you out of those wet clothes before you catch your death.”

She looked at him, puzzled. “Catch my death?”

Tom smiled as he led her toward his apartment. “Just a figure of speech. I’ve got a small washer and dryer in here. We’ll get your clothes dry in no time. In the meantime, I’ll wrap you in a warm blanket and make you some hot tea.”

She returned his smile and followed him without hesitation.

Inside, he handed her a blanket from his twin bed, showed her the bathroom, and told her to pass him her wet clothes when she was ready.

Within ten minutes, the clothes were tumbling in the dryer, and Sandra was curled up in the recliner, wrapped in the blanket, a steaming cup of tea cradled in her hands. Tom pulled a chair from the small table and sat across from her.

“Now… Sandra,” he began, “is it Sandra or Sandy?”

She tilted her head and gave a faint, impish smile. “I don’t know. Which one do you like?”

Amused, Tom studied her as the steam from the tea curled around her heart-shaped face. Her blue eyes shimmered like still water. “Let’s go with Sandra for now.”

She shrugged with innocent ease. “Okay.”

Tom leaned forward slightly. “Where are your things stored? What unit?”

He figured with a unit number, he could check her file in Angelo’s office and confirm her identity.

But Sandra’s expression turned uncertain. She shook her head. “I don’t know.”

Tom raised an eyebrow, mildly perplexed.

“But I think I can show you where my things are,” she added quickly, her voice hopeful.

Tom sighed, then nodded. “All right. As soon as your clothes are dry, you can show me. Sound good?”

Sandra nodded enthusiastically and settled deeper into the chair, sipping her tea as if the storm, the fear, and the confusion had all been washed away—for now.

Sandra sat quietly while Tom prepared more tea and waited for her clothes to finish drying. She had drawn her knees up to her chest again, just as she had in the lobby, and closed her eyes. A soft, folksy tune began to hum from her lips—something old and mellow, unfamiliar to Tom. The melody drifted through the apartment like a whisper, echoing off the walls and furniture as if the space itself were listening.

The dryer chimed, and Tom went to check it. Her clothes were warm and dry. He handed them to her and she disappeared into the bathroom to change.

Moments later, Sandra stepped out, fully dressed again, just as the phone in Angelo’s office began to ring.

Tom had reconnected the line after finding her, but now he hesitated. He knew what to expect—no voice, no explanation. Just the same persistent ringing.

Sandra turned toward him, her eyes wide with unease.

"Don't worry," he said gently. "There's no one there. Trust me."

She continued to stare, uncertain.

To reassure her, Tom walked to the office and picked up the receiver. As expected, silence greeted him. Then a click.

He glanced at the monitors. The compound was quiet. Empty. Rain still lingered, but there was no movement.

When he returned to the lobby, he was surprised to find Sandra standing at the door to the indoor facility, waiting. Her posture was calm, composed—her earlier fear replaced by something else. Something knowing.

He reached for the keys hanging by the office door.

"Was anyone there?" she asked, her voice light, her smile mysterious.

Tom paused, curious at the shift in her demeanor. "No. Just like I said. There's never anyone there when it rings."

Her smile deepened. "It got your attention though."

She stepped aside and gestured toward the door.

Puzzled, Tom unlocked it. As always, darkness loomed beyond. He stepped through cautiously, and the lights flicked on with a soft hum.

Sandra followed close behind as they made their way through the vast complex. Based on where the sedan was parked, Tom had a general idea of where her unit might be. When they reached the aisle near the far exit door, he turned to ask her to lead the way.

But she was gone.

He looked around, stunned.

Sandra had simply vanished.

Tom stood frozen, perplexed. Sandra couldn't have wandered far—not without him noticing. "Sandra," he called out, his voice echoing off the metallic walls. "Where did you go?"

No reply.

He turned left, then right. Looked ahead. Behind. Nothing. She had vanished.

He continued calling her name, his voice growing louder, more urgent, as he wandered up and down the aisle where he believed her unit to be. But every unit he passed bore a red lock—each one untouched, unopened. No one had rented a unit in this section for some time.

Then, without warning, the lights blinked off.

Darkness swallowed him whole.

Only the faint afterglow of white unit doors remained—ghostly outlines in the black. Even the window of the exit door gave off no light. It was like sinking into a murky sea, so thick and leaden he couldn't tell which way was up.

He reached out, searching for something solid. His hand found the cold, sterile surface of a unit door. He pressed against it, anchoring himself.

"Sandra!" he called, louder now. "Can you hear me? Are you lost? If you can hear me, come toward the sound of my voice!"

His words echoed into the void, swallowed by the vast emptiness. No reply. Only the low, mechanical hum of the facility—lifeless and unfeeling.

Tom began making his way back toward the office, trailing his hand along the unit doors to stay aligned. At the last moment, he chose a shorter route—an alternate path he rarely used.

He regretted it almost immediately.

Though shorter, the corridor was darker. The air felt heavier. As he plodded forward, the darkness seemed to press in on him, thick and suffocating. His breath grew shallow. He wasn't sure if it was fear or the weight of the blackness closing in.

"Sandra!" he called again, louder still. "Where are you?"

He hoped she had backtracked, maybe waiting near the office door, ready to guide him in.

Then he heard it.

A rattle.

The wire mesh above the units trembled—something was moving swiftly overhead. The clinking grew louder, more erratic, vibrating the mesh like a drum. It sounded like mandibles—large, jointed limbs—gripping the wire, dragging something heavy across the top.

Tom's heart seized.

He broke into a run, panic overtaking him. The aisle narrowed, and he found himself at a dead end. No way forward. No way back.

The rattling grew closer.

Closer.

Then—light.

A sudden beam spilled into the corridor from behind.

Tom turned and stumbled forward, collapsing into the lobby, caught in Angelo's grasp.

Chapter 4

Tom glanced at the clock on the wall—3:00 a.m.

Angelo sat at his desk, waiting patiently for Tom to gather himself. A fresh pot of coffee steamed between them, its strong aroma cutting through the haze of Tom's disorientation like smelling salts. Angelo looked as if he'd rolled straight out of bed—sweatshirt, faded jeans, mussed hair, and a face shadowed with stubble. For once, there was no unlit cigar in his hand.

"I called several times over the last half hour," he said, leaning back in his chair. "No one answered. I got worried and drove down to check on you."

He paused, then asked, "So, what's been going on? Why didn't you pick up?"

Tom shook his head slowly. "I've been trying to make sense of it all." His voice was low, uncertain. "There's something weird happening here, and I can't piece it together. I can't explain it."

Angelo sighed. “I told you—forget the detective act. You’re not here to chase ghosts. Just do your job and ignore the oddities.”

Tom slammed his cup down on the desk, frustration boiling over. “But it won’t let me leave it alone!”

Angelo frowned but didn’t react. He waited.

Tom threw his hands up. “The facility, Mr. Angelo! U-Lock’em! This place—it won’t let me ignore it. Every time I try, it rattles its cage louder. It wants something.”

Angelo’s expression remained unreadable.

“When the phone rings,” Tom continued, “I answer it. No one’s there. But it keeps ringing. Over and over. All night.”

He recounted the strange events—the outdoor units, the scooter, the rapping sounds, the flickering monitors. As he spoke, his eyes drifted to the screens again. The gold sedan was gone.

He paused, thoughtful. Then it hit him—before he’d led Sandra into the indoor facility, he’d glanced at the monitors. The sedan hadn’t been there.

Angelo shifted in his chair, glancing at the clock. “So, what’s wrong, Einstein? Let’s wrap this up. I’ve got to get home and get ready for work in two hours.”

Tom turned back to him, still perplexed. “Sandra’s car isn’t there anymore.”

At the mention of her name, Angelo sat forward abruptly. His eyes sharpened. “Did you say Sandra?”

Tom nodded.

“Do you personally know a girl by that name?” he asked.

Angelo’s face shifted—fear creeping into his features, as if he were bracing for something he didn’t want to hear.

“No,” Tom replied, puzzled by the question. “I just met her tonight. She came banging on the inside door around midnight, said she was lost and trying to find her storage unit. She was wet, scared. I tried to help her… but she vanished. Just like that. Into thin air."

Angelo's voice dropped to a whisper. "Did you say she was wet? Soaked?"

Tom nodded. "Yeah. Must've been from the storm. She was drenched."

Angelo sat back, mouth slightly open. For once, he had no clever comeback. No sarcasm. Just silence.

Tom leaned forward. "What's wrong?"

Angelo stood and began pacing, rubbing his hands together, glancing at the monitors as if expecting something to appear. After a minute, he stopped and turned. "What did the girl—Sandra—look like?"

His voice trembled slightly, as though he feared the answer.

Tom shrugged. "I don't know. Just a typical college-age girl. Eighteen, maybe nineteen. Blond hair. Striped top with thin straps. Faded jeans. Open-toed sandals."

He chuckled softly, almost to himself.

Angelo leaned over the desk, eyes sharp. "What's funny? Why did you laugh?"

Tom shifted, uneasy. "No offense. It's just… when I saw her face, she reminded me of a cartoon character. It struck me as odd at the time."

Angelo's gaze intensified, and Tom felt himself shrink under it.

"Who?" Angelo demanded. "Be specific."

Tom hesitated, then said, "Well… don't laugh. Her face was kind of pixie-like. Small nose, sparkling blue eyes, elfin ears. She reminded me of Tinker Bell. The Disney version."

Angelo straightened, eyes wide with a mix of astonishment and disbelief. He ran a hand through his already tousled hair.

Tom watched him closely. "Do you know this girl?"

Angelo didn't answer at first. He stared past Tom, as if searching memory for something buried deep.

Then, finally, he spoke. "Uh… no. Maybe."

Tom didn't press. He just waited.

And then, with quiet certainty, he said, "You know this girl. Don't you."

Angelo sank heavily into his chair, staring at the desk as if it held answers he didn't want to face.

Tom quietly stood, poured a fresh cup of coffee, and placed it in front of him. Angelo glanced at the cup and gave a silent nod of thanks. Tom returned to his seat.

"So," he said gently, "let's start from the beginning. It looks like you're more involved in all this than you've let on."

Angelo's eyes snapped up, sharp and defensive. "Watch it, Einstein," he growled. "Don't get too pushy. I hired you. You didn't hire me."

Tom backed off, sensing he'd crossed a line. He tried a softer approach.

"The other assistant managers you hired… they never told you why they quit. And they never came back. Is that true?"

Angelo didn't answer right away. Then he shrugged. "Maybe they mentioned a few oddities. Things that, to me, could be easily explained."

Tom nodded, pressing gently. "You said you stayed a couple of nights in the apartment between hires. And things happened you couldn't explain. But you stayed inside. You ignored it. Right?"

Angelo nodded absently, eyes distant.

"What kinds of things couldn't you explain?"

Angelo waved a hand dismissively, still avoiding eye contact. "Knocks on the wall. The sound of storage doors opening and closing. Lights flickering. The usual tripe."

Tom leaned forward. "Then why didn't you go out and investigate? Like I did?"

Angelo looked at him, voice firm. "Because it's trivial stuff. Easy to explain."

Tom's voice dropped to a whisper. "You were scared. You were scared then, and you're scared now. That's why you need assistant managers to stay here at night. You're too frightened to do it yourself."

Angelo's eyes narrowed. "Watch it, Einstein."

But Tom couldn't stop. He was close to something. "I think the others were scared too. That's why they left. But when I came, things escalated. Maybe because I was willing to dig deeper. I don't know."

Angelo slammed his hand on the desk. "You don't know what you're talking about! Maybe you should leave like the others."

Tom's eyes widened. "I remember you were surprised when I told you about the phone ringing with no one there. You said, 'That's a new one.' And when I told you about the kid running through the hole in the fence, you said, 'God, I've gotta fix that hole before it drives me crazy.'"

Angelo's voice was weak. "So?"

Tom stood, his voice steady. "I think you know it's all building toward something. You've felt it too. And I think you know something about that kid. You weren't annoyed by my story—you were haunted by it. That hole isn't just a nuisance.

It's a wound. And it's not me who's being haunted, Angelo. It's you."

Angelo suddenly stood, voice raised. "I don't have time for this nonsense. I need to go home and get ready for work."

He stormed toward the door, then stopped at the threshold, his back to Tom.

"Get your things together. I don't want you working here anymore. When I come back, I'll cut you a final check for the last few days."

He paused.

Then, quietly, almost to himself, he added, "I'm sorry."

And he left.

As the morning sun broke through the lingering clouds, the storm became a fading memory—its only remnants the wet pavement and the soft, rhythmic drip of water from the eaves. Angelo returned, dressed for work and carrying his briefcase as usual. He had shaved, combed his hair, and slipped into his standard uniform: khaki trousers, a dark blue polo, and black work shoes. He glanced briefly at Tom's packed belongings near the apartment door, then walked past without a word and closed himself inside his office.

Tom lingered at the counter, uncertain. Should he knock and ask for his severance check? Or wait? He decided to bide his time and tend to the morning's duties. A little extra money would help while he searched for something new.

Earlier, he'd thumbed through the want ads in the morning paper, jotting down a few possibilities. He folded the insert neatly and placed it on Angelo's desk—just in case.

An hour passed. Angelo remained behind the closed door.

In the meantime, Tom processed two new rental applications. Three regular customers came through the lobby, each having forgotten the door code. Tom recognized them, let them in, and reminded them of the digits. They nodded, offered quiet thanks, and moved on. He noticed they were warming up to him. That felt good.

He checked his watch—9:00 a.m.—then glanced again at the office door.

It wasn't until the mid-morning lull, around 10:00, that the door finally swung open. Angelo stood in the doorway and gave a silent wave, beckoning him inside.

Tom took his usual seat across from the desk. Angelo lowered himself into his chair with a wearied grunt, his face unreadable.

Tom waited.

Angelo leaned back in his office chair, studying Tom for a long, silent moment. Then he reached forward, picked up a check from the desk, and held it up.

"I thought it fair to pay you for a full day's wage today," he said, "along with the others."

Tom nodded his thanks and reached for the check, but Angelo pulled it back, just out of reach.

"Before you take it," he said, "I have something to tell you."

Tom settled back into his chair, sensing the shift in Angelo's usual overbearing demeanor.

Angelo placed the check in his lap and leaned back again, his voice low and deliberate. "I'm not trying to be dramatic," he began. "But I sat here a long time this morning, thinking about everything that's happened. Everything you said. And I'll admit it—you were right. I am scared. And I think I know who the girl is."

Tom remained quiet, expressionless. Inside, though, he felt a flicker of relief. Maybe even vindication. But he knew better than to interrupt. Angelo needed space to speak, to unburden himself. This wasn't a moment for gloating.

Angelo looked at him. "How old do you think I am?"

Tom shrugged. "I don't know… late thirties? Early forties?"

Angelo huffed. "You'd be surprised. I'm forty-nine. I'll be fifty next month."

He paused, gathering his thoughts. Tom didn't see the relevance, but he waited.

"Let me give you a little history," Angelo said. "About this facility. About the land. My family owned—still owns—most of the property on this side of the highway. The old homestead my great-grandfather built sat right about where we're sitting now."

Tom listened, the pieces beginning to shift.

"I inherited the land fifteen years ago, after my father passed. I'm an only child. No kids of my own. Back then, I was young, brash, full of vinegar. Thought I could turn anything into gold."

He leaned forward, voice soft. "I sold this part of the land to an investor who wanted to build storage units. Said it was a money maker—low overhead, easy to manage. I bought in. He owns the land, technically, but I'm a silent partner. The deal was simple: I sell the land, I get a cut of the profits, and a salary to manage it. I can stay on as long as I want. If I ever step down, I still get my share."

Angelo's voice grew more solemn, his eyes distant. "None of that is either here or there. I just wanted you to understand a little of the backstory. Why this place exists."

Tom nodded. "I understand. Take your time."

He regretted the words as soon as they left his mouth. They sounded too formal. Too confessional.

Angelo's eyes flashed briefly, but the edge faded. He sighed and stared off into the middle distance.

"I was in love once," he said quietly. Then he looked at Tom. "Can you believe that?"

Tom smiled. "Yes, I can."

Angelo continued as if he hadn't heard Tom's reply, his voice steady but distant.

"My father had a brother—my uncle—who used to visit the old homestead often when I was a kid. He'd bring his wife and his daughter from a previous marriage. She was about my age. Maybe a little younger. We were close. Out in the country, there weren't many neighbors, so we became each other's world."

He paused, eyes unfocused, lost in memory.

"We were young teens, thirteen or so, when we told each other we were in love. Made a pact not to marry anyone else." He smirked, but it didn't reach his eyes. "I know what people would say—puppy love. We didn't know what love was."

He looked at Tom, gaze intense. "But to us, it was real. And since then, I've loved no one else."

A long silence followed.

"And that girl's name was Sandra."

Tom sat wide-eyed, stunned. "But how… why?"

Angelo raised a hand. "I'm getting to that."

He took a breath, gathering the pieces of the story.

"Our property was big. We had a family cemetery behind the house. You could see the headstones from the kitchen window. There was a tornado shelter nearby, and an old well between the house and the cemetery. My grandparents used it back in the day. It was fenced off with wrought iron. The cemetery, I mean"

He paused again, the weight of memory pressing down.

"One day, our parents went to the market. Just a mile down the road. They figured they wouldn't be gone long, so they left us alone. We were old enough. But they told us to stay inside."

He shook his head. "We didn't listen."

"When we were young children, our favorite game was hide and seek. So, on a lark, we decided to play. I was 'it.' I started counting. Then I heard a scream."

Angelo's voice dropped to a mournful whisper.

"Sandra had decided to hide in the old well. She lowered the bucket down a few feet and tried to climb down the rope to sit on it. The crank lock held, but the rope couldn't hold her weight. It snapped. She fell."

He swallowed hard.

"They said she probably hit her head on the rocks and passed out before she hit the water. She drowned."

Tom stared at Angelo, eyes wide with sympathy. "Oh God, how tragic. I'm sorry."

Angelo exhaled slowly, the weight of memory pressing down. "Not as sorry as I was. I was just a kid—too shocked, too scared to know what to do. No adults around. Not enough rope to reach her. It was deep, a seventy-five-foot drop to the water."

He paused, voice growing quieter. "I called her name, hoping she'd answer. But she never did. It was too dark to see anything. It was like she'd vanished."

As Angelo spoke, Tom couldn't help but recall the Sandra he'd met—wet, disoriented, afraid of the dark. The resemblance was uncanny. The fear. The soaked clothes. The name.

"I searched everywhere for something—more rope, anything to tie together. But I was just a kid. I didn't know where my dad kept things like that. And even if I did, I doubt he had seventy-five feet of rope lying around."

Angelo gave a weary laugh. "I even thought about tying bed sheets together. But I didn't know knots. Didn't trust they'd hold. So, I sat there. On the grass. Crying. Waiting for our parents to come home."

He looked away, eyes distant. "They had to go to a neighbor miles away to get a rope long enough. My dad used the tractor to lower my uncle into the well. But they never found her. The well was deep. They figured she'd hit her head, passed out, and sank to the bottom."

He hesitated, then added, "That's why I asked if the Sandra you saw was wet. After the inquest, they ruled it an accident. Instead of dragging the depths, they filled in the well. Made it her grave. Put up a small plaque. Flowers."

Silence settled between them.

Then Tom spoke, voice low. "But how does that connect to the girl I met last night? She was probably soaked from the rain."

Without a word, Angelo opened his briefcase and pulled out a photograph. "I searched through some old albums in the attic," he said quietly. "Found this among them."

Tom took the photo and stared.

It showed a young girl, maybe thirteen, dressed in a pale Sunday dress—likely for Easter. Her straight blond hair framed a delicate face with a small nose and elfin ears. But it was the eyes that stopped him cold—sparkling blue, just like the girl he'd met last night.

His mouth fell open in astonishment.

When he looked back at Angelo, he saw a tear glistening at the corner of his eye. Angelo knew. Tom had recognized her.

"As kids," Angelo said, voice soft, "Sandra and I had a favorite toy—a scooter. We used to ride it together on the concrete roof of the huge tornado shelter. Around and around in circles. Mine's long gone now… and so was hers."

The pieces clicked into place.

"So, you believe the little girl I saw outside the night before last was Sandra," Tom said, "and the scooter was hers?"

Angelo nodded and gently took the photo back.

Tom's brow furrowed. "But why does she appear as both a young child and an older girl?"

"I don't know," Angelo admitted. "Sandra wasn't buried in the family cemetery, but it still stands—just beyond the fence near the dumpster. It's overgrown now. I haven't had the time or the heart to care for it."

He hesitated. "Some of the back outdoor units may be sitting on top of older graves. Maybe even the storm shelter."

Tom didn't speak. He let the weight of that settle.

"I know what you're thinking," Angelo said. "I should've exhumed the bodies. Moved them to a proper cemetery. But I was young. Brash. I didn't care. And now… I'm paying for it."

He looked at Tom, eyes heavy. "What I don't understand is why Sandra is at the center of it all. Is she trying to tell me something? Because I don't think she's the only one haunting this place."

He took a breath. "There's something else. Something darker. Haven't you felt it?"

Tom nodded slowly. "Yes. Even the Sandra I met last night was scared. There's something lurking in the shadows. And it's not her."

Angelo sat in silence for a long moment. Then he held up the check.

"I intended to let you go this morning," he said. "But the truth is—I need you. I need help solving this. I'd like you to stay, Tom. But I won't hold you here. If you want to leave, take the check. No hard feelings."

Tom was stunned. It was the first time Angelo had called him by name—not Einstein, not kid. Just Tom.

The request was sincere. And Tom felt it.

He nodded. "Yes. I'll stay and help you. I wouldn't miss it for the world."

Angelo smiled, tore the check in half, and dropped it into the trash.

Chapter 5

Before heading back home that morning, Tom discovered that Angelo had already made up his mind—he was staying the night, with or without him. It was clear he was desperate to get to the bottom of the mystery before it spiraled further. Tom watched as Angelo unloaded his car, surprised by the sheer volume of supplies: a suitcase packed for several nights, a folding cot with bedding, boxes of food, toiletries, and a scatter of odds and ends.

After stowing everything inside the studio apartment, Angelo turned to Tom. “Go home. Relax. Be back by 5:30,” he said firmly. “I’ll hold the fort and finish unpacking during the slow hours.”

Tom hesitated, reluctant to leave. But exhaustion tugged at him, and he agreed.

Driving home, his thoughts drifted to their shifting relationship. The haunting had drawn them closer, but now

Angelo seemed to be slipping back into his old self—guarded, skeptical, and just a little smug.

Earlier, while unloading the car, Angelo had tossed out a familiar jab. "Hope you don't mind the company, Einstein," he said. "I think it's important I see for myself if this haunting is real. After all, I only have your word that you saw Sandra—if it was really her."

The comment caught Tom off guard. It felt like backpedaling.

He'd stopped what he was doing and looked at Angelo. "Are you still unconvinced that the girl I met last night was Sandra? Or the little girl I saw with the scooter?"

Angelo shrugged, avoiding eye contact. "I guess I'm still hoping it's all just a misunderstanding. Something explainable. Or maybe Sandra's just… saying hello."

He turned toward the box at his feet and pulled out two walkie-talkies, fully charged. "That's why we both need to be here. We can cover both ends. Like when the outdoor units opened—you had to run back inside to check the monitors. They were closed, sure, but maybe someone shut them while you were gone. If two people were investigating, one could stay outside while the other watches the monitors."

Tom couldn't argue with the logic, but the tone grated. Angelo was playing it too cozy, too calculated—like he was trying to poke holes in Tom's experiences.

"See," Angelo said, holding up the walkie-talkies with a grin, "I may not be a college graduate like you, but I know how to think ahead."

Tom bristled. "I'm not an expert in ghost hunting, Mr. Angelo. I don't see it as a business. I'm not making it happen—it just happens. And it's scared me witless."

"Humph," Angelo replied, unconvinced. "Well, we'll see how it all shakes out, won't we? But hey, we can't expect Halloween every night."

As Tom drove away, he fumed. Angelo's cocksure attitude was back—and it was wearing thin.

The campus of Mid-State University lay tucked among towering pines and manicured shrubs, its blend of old federal architecture and modern redbrick buildings giving it a timeless, almost contemplative air. Crisscrossing sidewalks and narrow roads wound through the grounds like veins, connecting lecture halls, dormitories, and quiet courtyards. Though summer had stilled most of the academic pulse, the library and fiscal offices buzzed with year-round activity, their surrounding lots still packed with cars.

Tom didn't drive straight home. Something tugged at him—an urge to seek clarity, maybe even validation. He turned off the main road and wound his way through the sleepy campus, hoping to find Dr. Charles Merrick, his anthropology professor and trusted confidant.

The science building loomed ahead, a relic of the 1940s with its gray stone façade and metal flues jutting from the rooftop like sentinels. It stood in stark contrast to the sleek lines of the Fine Arts building nearby. Tom found a parking slot easily—summer rules were relaxed—and spotted Merrick's unmistakable dark blue Chevy, a vintage model from the 1960s, parked in its assigned space.

Inside, the building was hushed. Half the lights were off, the halls empty. Tom moved quietly through the corridor, the silence amplifying each footfall. At the end of the hall, the last office on the left glowed softly. The door was ajar, and through the gap,

Tom saw Dr. Merrick seated at his desk, pipe in hand, absorbed in a book on cultural ethnicity.

The professor's pipe, though unlit—thanks to campus smoking bans—was a fixture of his persona. He carried it like a badge of defiance, daring anyone to challenge his quiet rebellion. Tom had always thought Merrick resembled Dana Andrews, the rugged film star of the mid-20th century. Even now, at fifty-five, with gray creeping into his blond hair, Merrick retained a debonair charm that hadn't gone unnoticed by the female student body.

Tom paused at the door, unsure whether to knock or simply step in. The moment felt delicate, like the calm before a storm of revelations.

Tom knocked lightly on the door. Dr. Merrick looked up from his book, his expression brightening with recognition.

"Well, this is a pleasant surprise, Mr. Baker," he said, placing his unlit pipe in the ashtray. "I imagined you'd be busy working through the summer. What brings you here? Not just a social visit, I presume."

He gestured to the chair across from him, and Tom sat.

"As a matter of fact, Dr. Merrick," Tom began, "there's something I need to talk to you about… if you're not too busy."

Merrick closed his book and leaned back, pipe in hand again. "Of course," he said. "Sounds serious. I hope it's not about your matriculation. I'd hate to lose you—you've shown real promise in anthropology. Most students just take the course to check a box."

Tom waved a hand. "No, no. I'm not dropping out. And I'm not giving up anthropology."

Merrick nodded, chewing absently on the stem of his pipe. "Good. Then what's on your mind?"

Tom took a breath and began recounting the events of the past few days—the strange occurrences at the storage facility, the girl named Sandra, the scooter, the haunting atmosphere, and Angelo's confession. He spoke steadily, watching Merrick's face for any flicker of disbelief or judgment.

When he finished, Merrick sat quietly, as if waiting for more. Then he leaned forward, tapped his pipe in the ashtray out of habit, and sat back again.

"Is that all?" he asked.

Tom blinked. "Is that all? Isn't that enough? What do you think of the story I just told you?"

Merrick gave him a thoughtful look. "It's not a question of what I think, Tom. It's what you think. Do you believe the place is haunted? Do you believe you saw a ghost? I wasn't there."

Tom looked down at his clasped hands. "I don't know what I think."

Merrick leaned forward, spreading his hands. "Tom, you know as well as I do—hauntings and ghosts have been part of human culture for millennia. Every society, every belief system, has its own version. It's nothing to be ashamed of. Whether they're real or folklore, they reflect something deeper—something essential about the values and fears of that culture."

Tom looked up, confused.

Merrick softened his tone. "Here's what I'm trying to say. Whether the haunting is real or imagined, whether the ghost exists in the world or only in the mind—it's trying to tell you something. It's a message. And the message is always important."

Merrick leaned back in his chair, studying Tom with quiet intensity.

Tom finally looked up. "I expected you to solve my dilemma by simply telling me there's no such thing as ghosts." He gave his professor a quizzical look. "Are there? I mean… are ghosts real?"

Merrick chuckled, the sound low and thoughtful. "Yes… and no."

He set his pipe gently in the ashtray and folded his hands. "The scientific world doesn't acknowledge the supernatural—not because it's false, but because it's not natural. Science studies the natural world. It can't apply rigorous methodology to something that exists outside its framework. To the scientific mind, existence is what can be measured, observed, repeated."

He paused, then added, "But many cultures see existence as far more complex than what we can touch or test. We still struggle to understand the difference between the brain and the mind. Or what consciousness truly is—awareness, identity, soul, spirit."

Tom nodded slowly, absorbing the weight of the words. "But don't scientists today compare the brain to a digital computer?"

Merrick smiled. "Yes. And during the steam age, they thought the brain was like a hydraulic machine. We always try to explain the unknown using the tools of the known."

He shifted in his chair, leaning forward. "But you're missing the point. Stop trying to be scientific about what's happening at that quirky storage facility. You can't study it with instruments or equations—tools that can't be applied. Instead, use the tools of culture, of folklore, of memory."

He reached for his pipe and tapped the ashtray absently. "You can't reason with irrational patients in an asylum using logic. You have to understand what made them irrational. Their past. Their fears. Their stories. That's where the truth lives."

Tom nodded slowly, the pieces beginning to fit. "So, whether the haunting is real or imagined doesn't matter. What matters is understanding the land's history, the family's culture, the emotional residue. That's how we resolve it."

Merrick pointed with his pipe stem. "Exactly. But be careful. Don't let your own desires shape the narrative. That's the trap. We see it all the time with those ghost-hunting shows—'There must've been a murder here,' 'A restless spirit seeking revenge.' All that dramatic rot designed for ratings."

He leaned back again, eyes thoughtful. "You're not chasing a ghost, Tom. You're chasing meaning."

Tom sighed, shoulders heavy. "But how do I know the difference between what I want to believe… and what it wants me to believe? It's all so elusive. And I don't know the first thing about ghosts or hauntings."

Merrick placed his unlit pipe between his teeth and sat quietly for a moment, eyes narrowing in thought. "Let me tell you what I understand about hauntings and ghosts," he said at last. "Which, admittedly, is meager."

Tom leaned back, listening.

"One thing you need to understand," Merrick began, "is that hauntings are specific. Unique. You don't encounter the same ghost in a hundred different places. Especially not across cultures. Each haunting is tied to its own context—its own story."

He gestured with his pipe. "This Sandra specter you've seen—she's not random. She's tied to that location. Think of her like a tour guide at a historic site. She's showing you something. Offering clues. Trying to tell you why the place is haunted."

Tom frowned. "So, you mean the haunting centers around Mr. Angelo's family home?"

Merrick nodded, then raised a finger. “Yes—but don’t stop there. To truly understand the haunting, you have to look beyond the homestead. That land has history. People lived there long before Angelo’s family ever built a house. Their stories matter too.”

Tom nodded slowly, absorbing the layers.

“And on that note,” Merrick continued, “be aware—there may be other specters. Others who want to be acknowledged. Not all of them will be connected to Angelo’s bloodline. Sandra’s presence seems protective, yes. But you mentioned another force. Something darker. Something less… amenable.”

He leaned forward, voice low. “That kind of presence doesn’t just linger. It demands. It may be seeking justice. Or retribution. Or resolution.”

Tom sat in silence, the weight of the professor’s words settling over him.

“You mean,” he said quietly, “it could be dangerous?”

Merrick leaned forward, his voice low and reflective. “Possibly. But I’ve never known a ghost to actually harm anyone,” he said. “The real danger usually comes from within—fear, hysteria, the unraveling of the mind when faced with the unknown.”

Tom listened intently as Merrick continued, placing his unlit pipe between his teeth and speaking with quiet conviction.

“Most hauntings revolve around subtle, almost playful forms of communication. Odd sounds. Pungent odors. Flickering shadows. Eerie feelings. Soft whispers. A tap on the shoulder. They’re designed not to terrify, but to provoke. To prick the conscience. To nag at something buried. Like children playing harmless pranks on Halloween.”

He paused, then added, "Nothing about a haunting is ever conclusive. It's elusive by nature. Fragmented. It's meant to be pieced together—like a puzzle."

Tom nodded slowly, the tension in his chest easing just a little.

Merrick chuckled absently. "In a way, anthropologists work with ghosts all the time. When we study bones and artifacts, we're reestablishing a relationship with the spirits of a former culture. We're studying their ghostly remains, their habitats. And in doing so, we're changed. We learn where we came from."

He was quiet for a moment, lost in thought. Then he continued.

"As I mentioned before, let the ghost be your guide. But not those fanciful spirit guides mediums tout. It will reveal its needs in time. Maybe it wants to be remembered. Maybe it seeks acknowledgment. Or maybe it's satisfied simply by repeating its presence. Hauntings are often repetitive, after all."

He sighed. "You have your work cut out for you."

Tom stood, grateful for the insight. "Thank you for listening. And for the information. I wish you'd come out to the site and take a look for yourself. But I guess that's asking too much."

Merrick shook his head gently. "You don't need me. You've got a good head on your shoulders. Besides, I'm getting too old for field work. That's for the younger cadre now."

For a moment, he seemed to drift into thought, as if something had just occurred to him.

Tom noticed. "Did you think of something that might help?"

"I'm not sure," Merrick replied, tapping the tip of his pipe against his lip. "Tell you what—I'll make a few calls. See what I can dig up."

He took down Tom's home number and the contact for U Lock'em, then stood and extended his hand.

"Good luck to you," he said warmly. "And good hunting."

Tom shook his hand, feeling the quiet weight of the moment. Then he turned and stepped back into the hallway, Merrick's words echoing in his mind like distant footsteps in an old house.

Chapter 6

At the end of the workday, Angelo decided to split up the closing duties. He handed Tom a walkie talkie and sent him outside to check the perimeter while he took responsibility for the indoor facility. They were behind schedule—too much time spent setting up Angelo's overnight stay—and the sun had already slipped behind the trees, its filtered light casting a sickly yellow through the leaves.

Tom stepped out through the lobby door and into the deepening twilight. The sky had darkened to a rich cobalt blue, and shadows spread across the pavement like pitch. The exterior lights hadn't flickered on yet. The wind whipped through the smaller trees, their limbs flailing like skeletal arms trying to catch his attention.

From where he stood, the hole in the fence blended into the dark corner of the lot, and the dumpster loomed like a hulking mass without form. Tom waited for the automatic lights to snap on. Nothing. He checked his watch—6:45. They should've activated by now. He waited another five minutes. Still nothing.

With a sigh, he clicked on his flashlight and began his rounds.

The wind was brisk—too brisk. The lights were out. Everything felt off. It was all so cliché, he thought, like the opening scene of a horror movie. He tried to shake the feeling and focus on the task.

At each outdoor unit, he swept his light across the locks, checking for signs of tampering. The darkness thickened around him, falling like a curtain. The wind rattled the metal doors like empty cans and whistled through the compound, sending scraps of paper skittering across the pavement like frightened spirits.

He paused. The hole in the fence yawned beside it, darker than the night itself. His flashlight beam couldn't penetrate its depths. He scanned the area carefully. No scooter. A small wave of relief passed through him.

But as he turned back toward the units, something caught his eye—a shadow slipping through the far door of the facility. He couldn't make out who or what it was, but his stomach dropped. He knew, instinctively, that Angelo was the target tonight.

Tom pressed the button on the walkie talkie. "Mr. Angelo?" he called. No answer. He tried again. And again. Silence.

He broke into a slow jog toward the door, but the wind surged, pushing against him with unnatural force. If he were a kite, he'd have been airborne. He angled his body, veering toward the indoor structure, and pressed his back against the wall to block the gusts.

Then he heard it—a metallic rattle in the middle of the darkened pavement. It groaned and scraped like the door of an ancient dungeon. He swung his flashlight toward the sound.

The beam landed on a massive metal grate, slightly sunken into the pavement. A runoff drain for heavy downpours. But tonight, it looked like something else entirely—like a mouth waiting to open.

Tom's flashlight beam steadied on the grate.

He watched, breath caught, as one crusted corner lifted—just a half-inch—then dropped with a heavy, metallic clank. A chill crept up his spine. From the hole beneath came a deep, guttural huff, like something exhaling. Tom swore he saw the breath—misty, pale, rising from the darkness.

The grate shifted again, this time lifting higher, groaning under its own weight. It rose halfway before slamming back into place, the sound echoing across the lot like a warning.

Tom didn't wait.

He turned sharply, rounding the corner of the building, and sprinted toward the lobby entrance. His heart pounded against his ribs. He had no desire to find out what hovered beneath that grate—no interest in meeting whatever had stirred below.

The wind howled behind him, chasing him like a predator.

Angelo strolled jauntily down the aisleway, his unlit cigar clenched between his teeth like a stunted lance. He'd walked this circuit countless times before, and tonight, he was certain everything would be just as it always had been.

While Tom was away earlier that day, Angelo had taken time to reflect. He'd studied the situation more closely and come to a firm conclusion: all of it—the strange sounds, the flickering monitors, the scooter, the little girl, the young woman—was nothing more than the product of Tom's vivid imagination. And he, Jerry Angelo, had been swept up in the hysteria.

He admitted, grudgingly, that his past had made him vulnerable to suggestion—especially when Tom mentioned the girl. But not anymore. Tonight, he intended to prove it.

The facility hummed and ticked around him like a well-tuned machine. Exit doors were secure, storage units locked down for the night. Light sensors flicked off and on at expected intervals. The air conditioning throbbed steadily overhead, its cool breath circulating through the ducts. Every so often, a metallic pop echoed as the ducts expanded and contracted.

Angelo reached the final exit door and paused.

Suddenly, his walkie talkie crackled with static—then went silent. He pressed the button several times. Nothing. Dead batteries.

He turned toward the door, and without warning, the lights snuffed out—like candles blown by a sudden gust. Darkness fell around him like a cloak.

He blinked, trying to adjust. But the door was gone. The intersecting aisleway—gone. The storage units—gone. Even the path he'd just walked had vanished into black. He stood in a pitch-black void, the only certainty the smooth concrete beneath his feet.

He moved cautiously—one step in one direction, then another—hoping the motion would trigger the sensors. But the lights remained dead.

Disoriented, he cursed aloud. "Shit!"

As if in response, the A/C unit groaned to a halt. The hum of the facility died. Silence swallowed everything.

Fear crept in, slow and deliberate.

Angelo took a few deep breaths, trying to steady himself. "Okay," he said aloud, voice echoing faintly. "There's a logical explanation. A breaker tripped. A grid failure. Something simple."

He tried to orient himself. "I'm at an intersection. One way leads to the exit door—ten, maybe fifteen feet. Opposite that is the aisleway to the front. Beside me is the path I came from. And the other direction dead ends about twenty feet out."

He knew these facts. He'd memorized the layout. But in the dark, they meant nothing. He was lost in space.

There was only one option: pick a direction and walk until he hit something—a wall, a door, a unit. Anything.

And hope it wasn't something else.

Just as Angelo took a step, he heard a voice—soft, hushed—call his name.

He wasn't sure he heard it so much as felt it. It rippled through the air like a vibration in his bones.

He spun toward the sound.

At the far end of the aisleway—the one he'd just come from—a faint glow began to take shape. It was as if an actor had stepped into a stage lantern, bathed in soft lavender light. A figure emerged slowly, its form delicate and shifting.

"Jerry," the voice whispered. A soothing, siren call.

The sound carried like a wave through the silence, brushing against the walls and floor. Angelo's unlit cigar slipped from his teeth and landed on the concrete.

"Sandra," he breathed, barely audible. "It can't be."

The figure shimmered, shifting between the form of a child and a young woman. She stood motionless, as if speaking across a great chasm, her presence both familiar and otherworldly.

Then came a thump—deep and resonant—echoing through the A/C duct on the far side of the complex.

Angelo froze.

A moment later, he heard scurrying. Something was moving inside the ductwork, repositioning itself. He turned back to the apparition. She, too, had turned her attention to the sound. Her glow dimmed with fear.

Angelo remained still, afraid to breathe, afraid to move. Whatever was in the duct… it was hunting.

He began to ease toward the perimeter of the aisleway, inching away from the center. As if on cue, the entity surged through the ductwork, skittering like a massive spider, frantic and erratic. At one point, it raced toward him and stopped—just above his head.

Angelo dropped to the floor, cowering.

He lifted his head just enough to see the glowing specter vanish—snuffed out like the overhead lights. He pressed his cheek to the cool concrete, heart pounding.

The duct rattled again. The entity moved away and paused nearby. Then came a grunt, followed by the unmistakable sound of a vent being worked loose.

It had found an opening.

The vent grill broke free and clattered onto the wire mesh above one of the units, the impact sending a discordant vibration through the air. Angelo could only guess what followed. He imagined the entity squeezing through the opening, falling heavily onto the mesh, tearing it apart.

Then—thud.

A heavy body dropped into one of the empty units.

Angelo began crawling, desperate to reach a wall, a corner, anything. *I need to get away,* he thought, trembling.

Behind him, the entity slammed its hulking form against the unit door, trying to break through.

Angelo closed his eyes.

And waited.

At that instant, the overhead lights flickered back to life, casting a sterile glow across the aisle. The A/C roared awake, its hum filling the silence like a returning heartbeat.

Angelo didn't hear the monstrous entity anymore—only the faint, urgent voice of Tom.

"Mr. Angelo!" Tom called, sprinting toward him. "Are you alright?"

Angelo blinked, dazed, and slowly pushed himself up from the cold concrete. "I think so," he murmured, voice thin. He reached down and retrieved his stubbed cigar from the floor, brushing dust from his trousers and sleeves.

Everything looked… normal.

He glanced around, confused. The facility stood exactly as it had before the blackout. No signs of chaos. No broken vents. No torn mesh. No dented doors. *Did I dream it all?* he wondered.

He stepped toward the storage unit where he'd heard the entity slam against the door. He ran his fingers lightly over the surface—smooth. Untouched. He looked up. The A/C vent was intact. The grill in place. The mesh below undisturbed.

Tom watched him closely, concern etched across his face. "Are you okay? Is something wrong?"

Angelo turned to him, eyes distant, as if seeing Tom for the first time. He shook his head slowly, trying to clear the fog. "Yeah… I guess so."

He took one last look around, then sighed. "Let's get back to the office."

The rest of the evening passed without incident. No flickering lights. No strange sounds. No communication from Angelo.

He wore a stolid expression, his eyes glazed and distant, as if his thoughts were hopscotching across memories too tangled—or too personal—to share. When they returned to the studio apartment, he went straight to bed without a word. His body stretched across the cot he'd brought, back turned to Tom, facing the wall like a silent *Do Not Disturb* sign.

Tom left him to brood, deciding it was wiser to let sleeping bears lie. He flicked off the light and lay on his back, staring at the ceiling.

The soft glow from the bathroom nightlight began to seep into the bedroom area, casting faint shadows across the ceiling. Imperfections emerged from the dark—cobwebs hanging like wisps of cloud in the corner, a thin crack near the light fixture, and an old water stain near the bathroom wall. To Tom, the stain resembled a cartoon ghost—arms spread wide, two charcoaled eyes glaring down.

He looked away and turned on his side.

Sleep must have come quickly, because he woke with a start to the shrill ring of the office phone. The clock on the stove read 2:20 a.m.

Tom didn't move. He was used to this. The phone rang every night at the same time. And every night, there was no one on the other end.

After the tenth ring, Angelo mumbled from the cot, "Well, are you gonna answer it, Einstein? Or do you decide when to work and when not to work?"

The phone rang again.

"It happens every night," Tom replied quietly. "There's no one there." The familiar disturbance still made his skin crawl.

Two rings later, Angelo threw off his covers and stomped to the office, grumbling under his breath. Tom listened as the phone rang a few more times, then heard Angelo pick up.

There was a pause.

Then a muffled exchange—words Tom couldn't make out.

Seconds later, the receiver clattered back into its cradle, and Angelo shuffled back to bed.

Tom waited, afraid to ask. But certain of the answer.

Then Angelo spoke, his back still turned. "In case you're wondering if your spook called or not," he growled, "it was the police station checking on us. I asked them earlier to call and make sure we were okay."

A heavy pause followed.

"So much for your ghost theory, Einstein."

He said nothing more.

And the rest of the night remained quiet.

Not even a ghostly phone call.

The next day passed like a whisper.

Hardly anyone entered the compound—no new customers, no familiar faces—and the phone sat silent for hours. The sun gleamed in a cloudless sky, polished silver against the blue. The wind had vanished, and the tall green trees surrounding the property stood motionless, like sentinels guarding a forgotten fortress.

Tom and Angelo moved through their duties with barely a word exchanged. Even with little to do, they found ways to stay apart. Tom knew Angelo was still brooding over the previous night's encounter, and he didn't press. Angelo, for his part, never asked Tom what he had seen.

To complicate matters, both the entrance and exit gates malfunctioned. The entrance gate had to be forced open and left that way, allowing anyone to come and go freely. A repair crew wouldn't arrive until the next day, which only added to Angelo's simmering frustration. Tom could almost hear his teeth grinding behind the closed office door.

With the gate wide open, Tom stayed vigilant. He made frequent rounds, checking locks, inspecting doors, scanning corners where someone might hide. The compound felt exposed, vulnerable.

Mid-afternoon, after one of his rounds, Tom stepped into his studio apartment to grab a bottle of water from the fridge. He twisted off the cap and took a long, cool drink.

Then he heard it—the soft click of the lobby door opening and closing.

He set the bottle down and stepped into the lobby.

A young woman stood at the counter.

She was petite, her shoulders barely rising above the countertop. Her wavy blond hair framed a face that seemed to glow with quiet grace. She wore a semi-business suit: a crisp white blouse beneath a dark green jacket. Her eyes, sky-blue and clear, seemed unfocused—until Tom appeared at the counter. Then she smiled, and her dimples smiled with her.

"Hello," she said, her voice light and warm.

Tom returned the smile, assuming she was a new customer. "Hello. Can I help you? Looking to rent a storage unit? We've got a few specials running. What size are you looking for?"

He reached beneath the counter for a rental application.

But she shook her head gently. "Oh, I'm not here to rent a storage unit."

Her smile lingered, soft and knowing.

"Oh?" Tom asked, glancing toward Angelo's closed office door. "Then what are you here for?"

"I was sent to help you," she said simply, as if that explained everything.

Tom studied her, uncertain. "Help me?" he echoed. "Help me do what?"

Her expression didn't change. Her voice remained calm.

"To catch a ghost."

At that moment, Tom heard a soft rustle near the young woman's feet. She lifted a leash, and a Golden Retriever stepped around to her other side, sitting obediently with a wide, panting grin—the kind only dogs could manage, tongue pink and lolling.

Tom quietly returned the unfilled application to the stack beneath the counter. He stared at the woman, nonplussed, unsure how to respond.

"I don't think I follow," he said slowly. "You were sent to me… to catch a ghost?"

She nodded, still smiling. Then her expression shifted slightly, as if a realization had just clicked into place. "Ah," she said, "you didn't know I was coming, did you?"

Tom gave a faint, almost imperceptible shake of his head. But she continued to look at him, waiting for a response. His gesture didn't seem to register.

Then he glanced again at the dog, and it hit him—she was blind. The Golden Retriever was a guide dog, just like the ones he'd read about.

"I'm sorry," he said, flustered. "I didn't realize you were… you know…"

She chuckled, light and unbothered. "Blind, you mean."

Her ease disarmed him. Despite his embarrassment, he nodded and quickly corrected himself. "Yeah."

She carried herself with poise and quiet confidence. Switching the leash to her other hand, she extended her right hand above the counter. "Why don't we start from the beginning? My name is Claire Webber."

Tom hesitated, still trying to catch up. He looked at her hand, then at the dog, then back at her face. She kept her hand extended, waiting patiently.

Finally, he reached out and shook it. "Tom Baker. Pleased to meet you."

Her hand was warm and soft, limp in his grasp like a mitten-shaped leaf. She shook with her thumb curled inside his palm, like a child not yet taught the formalities of a handshake. Yet her face and demeanor betrayed no shyness—only grace.

"Ah! So, you're Tom Baker," she said, as though she'd been expecting him.

Tom crossed his arms, still wary. "How do you know me? And what is this all about?"

Claire laughed, the sound bright and unassuming. "It's no mystery, Mr. Baker. We have a mutual friend—Professor Merrick at Mid-State U."

Tom's arms dropped in astonishment. "You know him?"

"As a student," she replied, still smiling. "I've taken a couple of his courses. He's also good friends with my employer, Beth Wimberly—of Wimberly Realtors."

Tom struggled for a proper response. "I'm not sure how you can help us. I mean… me."

Claire wasn't fazed by the dodge. Her smile remained steady. "You really mean *us*. I already know about the issue. It includes you and your manager."

She turned her head slightly, scanning the office with a gaze that made Tom question her blindness. "Is there a place we can talk more privately? I promise not to keep you from your work if you need to step away."

Tom glanced at Angelo's closed office door, then back to her. "Sure. We can talk in here." He gestured toward his apartment door, then caught himself. "I mean, inside my studio apartment."

She nodded, took hold of the dog's harness, and gave a soft command. "Forward, Chaucer."

Tom blinked at the name. *Chaucer?* Strange name for a dog, he thought.

The Golden Retriever guided her smoothly around the counter and through the apartment door with practiced ease. Once inside, Claire pointed toward the table. "Is that someplace we can sit?"

Bemused, Tom nodded. "Yes."

Chaucer led her to the chair. With one hand, she found the edge of the table; with the other, she pulled out the chair and gently felt the seat before sitting down.

Tom took the chair across from her as Chaucer curled up beside her feet.

"I was under the impression you're blind," he said cautiously. "But you seemed to use vision to find your way in, locate the table, and sit."

Claire smiled, glancing at her hands before lifting her sky-blue eyes to meet his. "I'm not totally blind. I can see some things—provided there's enough light and the space isn't too cluttered."

She looked around the apartment. "You keep it well-lit here, and it's small, not crowded. I also have a mental map of how things generally look, so I can identify them even if I can't see the details."

Tom leaned in, intrigued.

"Tables are usually round or rectangular. Chairs are easy to spot." She pointed behind him. "That's a refrigerator." She turned slightly and pointed again. "I'm fairly certain that's a television with a leisure chair facing it." Then she gestured toward the beds. "And those must be yours and your manager's."

Facing Tom again, she smiled. "Now that we've got that out of the way, why don't we jump into the heart of the issue? Tell me what's going on here."

Tom hesitated, then asked, "Wait. How is it that you're blind… but able to be a medium?"

Claire took a breath, her expression calm.

"Easy," she said. "Because I'm not a medium."

Tom cocked his head, trying to make sense of it. "Don't mediums communicate with ghosts… the spirit world, I mean? Isn't that why you're here?"

Claire shook her head gently. "I don't really communicate with ghosts. I just see them. Sometimes I hear what they say, but I don't think they're trying to send messages to *me*. It's usually the other person—someone like you—they're trying to reach."

Tom frowned, perplexed. "So, what do you do then? What's your role in all this?"

For the first time since they'd met, Claire seemed a little unsure. Her voice softened. "I don't know. I guess it's a learning experience for me too."

Then she brightened, her poise returning. "You could think of me as a kind of consultant. In many cases, I'm able to intuitively help piece together why someone is haunted. What the connection is. What the ghost might be trying to resolve."

Tom hesitated. "So, you don't pick up vibes… or energy?"

Claire blinked. “Yes, but not like you see on television. Mediums on TV walk into a room and immediately know how many ghosts are present, who they are, what they want. That’s not me. I don’t summon them. I don’t chase them. I just… run into them. When they want to be seen.”

A quiet lull settled between them.

Then Claire leaned forward slightly. “So, why don’t we get down to it. Tell me what’s been going on.”

Chapter 7

For the next thirty minutes, Tom laid out the strange events of the past few nights to Claire—every unsettling detail, every flicker of doubt, every moment that had left him questioning reality. When he finished, Claire sat quietly, her head tilted slightly, her expression thoughtful.

"I can tell by your voice and body language that these experiences have really shaken you," she said gently. "But what's odd is that, based on your account, you're not the center of the haunting. Your manager is. What's his name again… Jerry Angelo?"

"Did I hear my name?"

They both turned at once.

Angelo stood in the doorway, eyes hooded, a stack of papers in one hand. He glanced between them, then pulled his unlit cigar stump from his mouth and pointed it toward Claire. "Who's this?"

Caught off guard by his sudden appearance, Tom stumbled over his words, but Claire stepped in smoothly.

"I'm Claire Webber," she said with a warm smile. "I'm interested in renting a unit here."

Angelo narrowed his eyes. "Then why are you in his apartment? Customers aren't allowed behind the counter. You know that, Tom." He turned to Claire. "No offense, Miss."

"None taken," Claire replied graciously. "But please don't blame Mr. Baker. He offered to interview me in a space that would better accommodate my blindness."

Angelo's gaze lingered on her, skeptical. But when he noticed the dog at her side, the harness gave a clear indication, he grunted in reluctant approval. He stepped to the counter and pulled a blank application from the stack.

"Well then," he said, handing it over, "you'll probably need this too."

"Oh, yeah," Tom said, sheepishly. "I guess we do." He stood, rubbed his palms on his pants, and took the form.

Angelo studied him for a moment. "I've got a visitor stopping by in about thirty minutes. I'll need your help when he gets here."

Tom nodded. "We should be done by then."

Angelo turned to Claire and gave a curt nod. "Welcome aboard, Miss Webber."

Then he disappeared into his office, the door clicking shut behind him.

Tom waited until the sound of the door settled, then leaned toward Claire and whispered, "Thanks. I appreciate you backing me up like that."

Claire gave him a knowing smile. “I could tell you didn’t want him to know why I was really here. And now I see why. He’s a bit of a grump.”

Tom glanced toward the office door. “Don’t let him fool you. He’s sharp. Sharp as a razor. I’d better fill out this application while we talk. He’ll probably check it later.”

Claire nodded. “You never said why you’re so bothered by all this—especially since it’s your manager who seems to be the focus.”

Tom slowly filled in the blanks on the form, his pen moving with deliberate care. “At first, I thought it was me. I mean, I was the one seeing things. Hearing things. But the more I paid attention, the more I realized it was Mr. Angelo. He’s the one being haunted. He just refuses to admit it.”

He paused, then added, “I think deep down, he knows it’s real. But he’s doing everything he can to convince himself otherwise.”

Claire handed Tom her identification card, the address printed clearly beneath her name. He examined it, eyebrows raised.

“This looks like a driver’s license,” he said. “How do you have one of these?”

“Blind people need IDs too,” she replied with a gentle smile. “The same place that issues driver’s licenses also provide identification cards for non-drivers.”

Tom nodded, jotting down the information. “I’ll need a phone number too. Do you have a cell?”

She shook her head. “Just a landline.” She gave him the number.

As he filled in the application, she clarified, “So what you’re saying is—Mr. Angelo is in denial. And the reason so much of this has happened to you is because you're being used as a conduit to reach him."

Tom paused, pen hovering over the page. "Possibly," he said. "The problem is, I'm not sure I believe in ghosts."

He stared at the form, then added, "It's strange. I don't believe in hauntings, but I've come face to face with something. And Angelo—he *does* believe, deep down. But he's doing everything he can to deny it."

Claire nodded, her expression unreadable.

Tom returned her ID card and stood. "We need to pick out a unit for you to rent—or at least go through the motions."

Claire rose, snatching up Chaucer's leash. "By all means. I need to walk through the area you say is haunted anyway."

At the door to the indoor facility, Tom hesitated. "I thought you said you weren't a medium. Don't mediums need to walk through haunted areas to get a reading or pick up vibes?"

Claire laughed. "I assure you, I'm not a medium, Tom. I just want to experience the space firsthand. If I do pick up anything… it'll be unexpected."

Just then, the front door burst open.

A tall man with salt-and-pepper hair and a dark mustache strode in, followed by another man carrying a video camera and recorder. The first man stepped to the counter with an impatient air.

Tom called out, "I'll be with you shortly. I just need to show this customer around."

The man glanced at his watch, exasperated. "If you must," he said, his voice tinged with a foreign accent. "But I'm pressed for time. Do it quickly."

Tom frowned at the man's haughty tone. "If we're not back soon, you can ring the bell on the counter. My manager can assist you."

As Tom and Claire stepped through the door to the indoor complex, the bell rang—sharp and insistent.

Claire felt a tremor ripple through her as she stepped deeper into the vast, echoing interior of the storage complex. Even with her limited vision, the place overwhelmed her. Every aisle looked the same—rows of identical storage units, each door a mirror of the last. The exit doors were spaced with mathematical precision, indistinguishable from one another. There were no landmarks, no irregularities to anchor her. The symmetry was oppressive, disorienting.

It gave her the creeps.

Even the sounds betrayed her. The constant drone of the A/C system masked the subtle echoes she usually relied on to gauge space and distance. The usual cues—shifts in air pressure, the bounce of her voice—were swallowed by the mechanical hum. She was left to depend entirely on Chaucer and her meager residual vision, which offered only vague outlines and shadows.

"Is it all like this?" she asked, her voice tight with unease.

Tom, a few steps ahead, turned to face her. "Just about," he said. He pointed toward the far end of the building. "Over there, there are no windows or doors at all. The roof's higher, too. With no exits, it's pitch black. Even I don't like going over there."

Claire shivered, and she felt Chaucer shift uneasily beside her. But it wasn't a ghostly presence that unsettled them—it was the sheer, inhuman uniformity of the place.

As they circled the outer aisles, Tom explained the layout and the lighting system. Motion sensors triggered the lights, flicking them on and off as they passed. Even in daylight, the cavernous space was cloaked in shadow. The overcast sky outside only deepened the gloom. Claire could barely imagine what it must feel like at night.

They passed the final exit door and turned up the far aisle when a voice cut through the mechanical hum.

"Mr. Baker! If you're in here, I need you in my office ASAP!"

Angelo's voice rang out, sharp and commanding. A moment later, the slam of the metal door echoed through the complex like a gunshot.

Tom winced. He turned to Claire. "I need to get back. Maybe we can finish the tour later?"

Claire hesitated, then said, "Why don't I just stay here for a bit?"

Tom studied her. "Are you sure you're okay in here by yourself? You seemed kind of nervous earlier."

She forced a smile. "I'll be fine. Just tell me how to get back, and I'll meet you at the office."

He gave her a long, reluctant look. "Alright. Just keep going straight down this aisle about 75 feet or so. When you reach the next cross-aisle, turn right."

Claire swallowed. "Oh my… these aisles are long."

"They are," Tom agreed. "You sure you'll be okay?"

She nodded, offering another faint smile. "I'll be fine."

Tom turned and jogged off toward the office, disappearing around a dim corner. She saw his shape vanish in the shadows; shadows that seemed to press in just a little closer, and the hum of the A/C felt heavier—like a breath held in the dark.

Like clockwork, the lights remained brilliantly lit as Claire made her way down the aisle, Chaucer guiding her with quiet diligence. But the deeper she walked, the more the sameness of the place began to unravel her sense of direction. Every unit looked identical. Every aisle mirrored the last. There was nothing to orient her—no landmark, no variation. Just endless symmetry.

She began to lose track of how far she'd gone. The distance Tom had described blurred in her mind.

Then Chaucer whimpered.

His tail, which had hung low the entire walk, tucked tighter against his haunches. Claire noticed the lights had begun to dim—subtly at first, then more rapidly. Within moments, she was swallowed by total darkness.

She glanced behind her. No light from the exit door. No glow from the overhead fixtures. Just black.

She froze.

Claire knew this feeling. Something was about to happen. Her heart pounded against her ribs, her breath quickened. Chaucer pressed against her leg, trembling. She closed her eyes and took slow, steady breaths, trying to calm the storm inside her.

When she opened them, the darkness had changed.

A scene resolved in front of her—foreign, vivid, and impossible.

A fire burned in the near distance. Not large, but bright. A man crouched beside it, palms outstretched toward the flames. His skin was dark, sunburned and leathery. He wore no shirt, only a necklace of beads and bones. His straight black hair hung limp over his shoulders and chest. His face was painted green, with long black streaks encircling his eyes and trailing down his cheeks, disappearing beneath his chin.

A dark linen band wrapped his forehead, and atop his head sat a headdress—a massive black bird, its wings spread, its lifeless beak frozen in a perpetual screech.

He wore a loincloth and sandals made of animal hide.

The entire tableau was hideous. Frightening.

Claire didn't understand how she could see it so clearly. Her usual blurred vision had sharpened, as if she were looking through a different lens—one not bound by the physical world.

As she shifted slightly, the man's eyes turned toward her. He rose slowly to his feet, arms hanging at his sides. He squinted, cocking his head in curiosity.

Claire remained still.

Chaucer whimpered again, trying to back away. Claire held him close.

The man's attention snapped to the dog. He grunted, low and guttural.

Then Claire heard a sound to her right—a flash of movement. The man turned his head sharply, tracking it.

He growled and unleashed a stream of words in a language Claire had never heard. Harsh. Ancient. Condemning.

He pointed at her, screaming now, his voice rising in fury.

Then he turned toward the darkness beyond the fire.

It was as if he gave a command.

From the shadows, a pair of glowing eyes emerged—yellow, wide, and unblinking. A tremendous huff echoed through the space, and the eyes shifted toward the man.

Claire instinctively stepped back, her breath caught in her throat.

Something was coming.

The man pointed again—this time directly at Claire and Chaucer.

The glowing eyes shifted, locking onto them.

Claire wanted to run, but she didn't know where. The symmetry of the complex had erased her sense of direction. As she turned away from the firelit scene, she heard the beast shuffle toward them—heavy, deliberate.

She let out a piercing scream.

Suddenly, the lights snapped on.

Voices echoed from the distance, casual and human. Claire spun around. The fire, the painted man, the monstrous eyes—gone. As if they'd never been there.

Not wanting to linger, she commanded Chaucer forward and turned down the intersecting aisle toward the office. At the far end, she saw figures moving, talking in low voices. As she drew closer, she recognized Tom, Angelo, and the foreign gentleman from earlier. Behind them, a man with a camera was filming the ceiling and aisles.

Their conversation stopped as she approached.

Angelo spoke first. "Miss Webber. Have you found a unit you liked?"

Tom remained silent, his eyes flicking to her with concern.

Claire shook her head.

The man with the foreign accent turned, his tone clipped and dismissive. "Who is she? Is she part of this investigation?"

"No," Angelo, clearly irritated by the man's disclosure, replied smoothly. "She's just a new customer looking to rent."

The man raised his eyebrows. "Good. I cannot have interference during my reading." He turned away, scanning the space with theatrical intensity.

"Miss Webber," Angelo continued, unfazed, "this gentleman is Pond Darogas, a renowned spiritualist. He's worked with law enforcement on several cases."

Claire tilted her head, feigning surprise. "Oh? Is the place haunted? Maybe I shouldn't rent a unit in a haunted facility."

Angelo waved a hand. "I assure you, Miss Webber, it's a minor—if nonexistent—issue. No property has been vandalized or disturbed."

Claire turned to Darogas, her voice light. "Perhaps you've worked with an acquaintance of mine—Detective Sergeant Lyles?"

Darogas gave her a long, appraising look, then sneered at Chaucer. "Ah, yes. A most tedious man. He refused my assistance when the department offered it."

"I see," Claire said, her tone knowing. She smiled at Tom, who stood quietly, shoulders slightly hunched.

She had seen something. And whatever it was, it wasn't going to be dismissed with a wave of the hand.

As though robbed of the spotlight, Darogas scowled, his voice sharp and theatrical. "I said I need no interference while I'm investigating. That means silence!"

With dramatic flair, he raised his hand and whispered, "I feel the presence of several individuals here."

He paused, eyes closed in deep concentration, then pointed down one aisle. "There is a young boy standing next to a unit, pleading for help." He shifted his hand slightly. "And just beyond him—a large man in dark clothing. He holds a knife. His eyes are fixed on the boy."

Tom glanced at Claire. She shook her head, expression flat. Angelo, however, was transfixed.

"Let us proceed!" Darogas commanded, striding forward with purpose. His cameraman scrambled to keep up, lens trained on his face. Angelo followed, eyes wide, leaving Tom and Claire trailing behind.

As they moved deeper into the complex, Claire leaned toward Tom and whispered, "This man is a fraud."

Tom nodded. "I figured from your look."

"He's a professional psychic," she said. "Maybe he sees something. Maybe not. But he's embellishing now—trying to make himself seem credible."

Tom looked at her. "How can you tell?"

Claire sighed. "The ghosts he described back there? Made up. Chaucer didn't react. He always senses them before I do."

Tom hesitated. "Did you see something after I left?"

Claire gave a solemn nod. "We'll see if he picks it up on the other side of the complex."

She said no more.

As they rounded the far aisle, Tom and Claire caught up. Darogas continued his performance—eyes closed, hand raised, pausing at intervals like a conductor waiting for the next note.

Then, as he approached the area where Claire had seen the ominous figure, he stopped.

"Ah!" he declared. "I feel a surge of energy nearby."

He crept forward, the cameraman capturing every twitch of his face.

"What do you see?" Angelo whispered, clutching his unlit cigar.

Darogas froze.

His hand dropped. His eyes widened.

Claire glanced at Tom and nodded.

"What's wrong?" Angelo asked, voice low and eager. "What do you see?"

Darogas turned slowly, lips trembling. Then he forced a smile. "Nothing," he said in a harsh whisper.

He signaled for the camera to shut off.

Without another word, he turned and strode toward the office exit. Angelo followed, confused.

"Nothing?" Angelo repeated.

Darogas didn't slow. "Nothing."

Angelo's voice rose, frustration bubbling. "But what about the little boy? The man with the knife? The others?"

At the office door, Darogas paused. He looked back at Angelo, eyes cold.

"They are of no consequence," he said. "Just spirits passing through. They have no relevance to this place."

He waved a dismissive hand, signaled to his cameraman, and they were gone—out the door before Angelo could say another word.

Chapter 8

Dejected, Angelo wandered into his office and dropped heavily into his chair. His eyes were glazed, distant—like someone staring through a fog only he could see.

Tom and Claire lingered at the doorway.

"Are you okay, Mr. Angelo?" Tom asked softly.

Angelo didn't respond at first. Then, as if snapping out of a trance, his usual bluster returned. "What makes you think I'm not, Einstein?" he growled.

He snatched a stack of papers from his desk and tossed them aside with a sharp flick. His glare returned to Tom. "So, what do you want? Don't you have work to do?"

Tom nodded and began to turn away, but Angelo's gaze shifted—finally noticing Claire.

"And what is it *you* want, Miss Webber?" he asked, still bristling. "Are you here to check on my welfare too?"

He stood abruptly, eyes darting between them. "Why are you *really* here, Miss Webber? Is it to rent a unit?"

There was a moment of hesitation.

"No," Claire said calmly. "I'm not here to rent a unit, Mr. Angelo. And please—just call me Claire."

Angelo's eyes continued to toggle between the two, suspicion mounting. "Einstein, will you *please* tell me what's going on before I toss the both of you out?"

Claire stepped forward, guiding Chaucer gently into the room. She spoke with quiet assurance. "I'm here to help you and Tom resolve your issue with your ghost."

Angelo stared at her, unmoving. "How do you know about our ghost?"

Claire chuckled. "Apart from watching your psychic muddle through his performance, you admitted the place was haunted."

"I said it *could* be haunted," Angelo snapped. "I never said *I* had a problem with a ghost."

He glanced at Tom, who stood frozen at the door, looking every bit the traitor.

Tom stepped inside, bracing for the worst.

Claire sighed and settled into a nearby chair, Chaucer curling beside her. "No," she said gently. "I knew before I came. And don't blame Tom—he was just as surprised to see me as you were."

She explained briefly how Dr. Merrick had contacted her, and who she was.

Angelo sat back in his chair, trying to piece it all together. Then he pointed at them. "Are you both taking archaeology classes together?"

"It's anthropology," Tom corrected, a little too quickly. "And no—we've never met before today."

He felt the tension rising, certain Angelo was about to fire him…again.

But Claire's voice cut through, low and baleful. "And I have to tell you—you have a bigger problem with ghosts than just a young girl."

Angelo's eyes narrowed. He leaned forward, squinting at her.

"What do you mean by 'bigger problem'?"

Claire drew in a breath and let it out slowly. "What your professional psychic, Mr. Darogas, probably perceived at the last moment—but failed to tell you—is that this job is dangerous. More dangerous and more complex than he expected."

Tom eased into the chair beside her. "What do you mean?"

She glanced from Tom to Angelo, her voice steady. "Mr. Darogas likely has some psychic ability. But it's either limited… or he's too frightened to use it when things get truly dark. I think it's both. On the far side of the complex, he picked up a presence—a real one. Something powerful. Something evil. And when he did, he bolted."

Angelo leaned back in his chair, the bravado draining from his face.

Tom spoke up. "So, he sensed what you told me you sensed earlier?"

"Yes," Claire said. "But I didn't just sense it. I *saw* it."

The tension in the room thickened. Angelo leaned forward, his voice cracking. "What did you see… Miss Web—Claire?"

Tom watched as Angelo's fear returned.

Claire described the vision in detail—the fire, the painted man, the headdress, the beast in the shadows. Her voice was calm, but the imagery was chilling.

Angelo sat in stunned silence.

"How can you see all that when you're… you know…" he finally asked.

"Blind?" Claire offered, gently.

He nodded, embarrassed.

She shrugged. "With my special vision—my ability to see the spirit world—I sometimes see more detail than I do in the physical world. But not always."

She let that settle.

"The movement that drew the man's attention—and mine—was probably Sandra. I don't know all the whys or hows, but I believe she's been held captive by this spirit and his familiar since her death. Somehow, she escaped. She's hiding. That's why she's reached out. That's why she's afraid."

"His familiar?" Tom asked.

Claire nodded solemnly. "The beast. The creature in the dark. It's bound to him—controlled by him. Like a witch with a black cat. It does his bidding. Although, I wonder if it may be the other way around—the familiar…or, perhaps, a demon, controlling him."

Tom's mind raced. He recalled the creature he'd heard behind the dumpster. The metal grate being lifted. The heavy thud.

"Oh my God," he whispered.

Angelo stirred from his daze, voice rising. "Wait—wait a minute! You're telling me Sandra's been held captive all these years and *now* she wants help? That's crazy!"

Claire reached down, brushing Chaucer's fur, her eyes unfocused but steady. "Time in the spirit world isn't measured like ours." She quoted softly, "With God, a day is like a thousand years, and a thousand years like a day."

Angelo scoffed. "What's God got to do with this?"

Claire scratched behind Chaucer's ears, her voice barely above a whisper. "Everything. The spirit world is where He resides… as well as other powers."

A chill crept up Tom's spine.

Something ancient was stirring.

As the sun sank below the tree line, casting long shadows across the compound, the three walked slowly around the perimeter—Claire and Chaucer in the lead, Tom and Angelo trailing behind. The doors to the outdoor units stood stolid and unmoving, like sentinels watching without eyes. The wind had died, and the cicadas had begun their whirring chorus in the trees, announcing the arrival of night.

Tom felt it now—night wasn't just the absence of sunlight. It was something else. Something older.

Claire's voice broke the silence as they walked. "Dr. Merrick did some digging into the history of this area. He found mention of a unique tribe of Native Americans—or Aboriginals, as he called them—who may have lived right here. Their history is vague, but they were distinct. Other tribes shunned them. Feared them."

She paused, letting the weight of that settle.

"The tribe's name was never spoken. Never written. Out of fear. But they were ruled by a shaman—an evil one. He practiced bad medicine. They say he could summon demons. And those demons demanded sacrifices… human sacrifices."

Tom frowned. "That doesn't sound like Native American tradition. They weren't like the Incas or Aztecs."

"True," Claire said. "But Dr. Merrick believes the sacrifices were more like warrior rituals—torture, like the Comanche and other tribes practiced. They believed they could absorb power from a conquered enemy. That kind of violence seemed to please the demons."

They walked a little farther before Claire continued. "Eventually, the tribe rebelled. They overthrew the shaman and scattered, mixing with other tribes. But the shaman stayed. Still worshipping the demons he'd called. No one knows what happened to him. But Dr. Merrick said he wouldn't be surprised if the shaman lived—and died—on the very land where this facility now stands."

She stopped just before the dumpster.

"I believe the man I saw in my vision was that shaman. An evil sorcerer, really."

Angelo's voice was low, uncertain. "So, if all this is true… why is he haunting us now? And what does it have to do with Sandra?"

Claire grinned faintly. "Ah, that's the crux of it, isn't it? And the very thing we need to find out."

At the dumpster, her attention shifted. Chaucer moved forward, tail low, sniffing the ground near the fence line. Claire reached out, hands extended, and found the hole in the fence. As her fingers traced its edges, Chaucer whimpered.

She examined the opening carefully. "Why is this hole here?"

She turned to Angelo. In the fading light, his face was pale.

"I don't know," he said, voice thin. "It was there when the facility was completed."

Claire gave him a long, quizzical look, but let it go. Chaucer seemed relieved to guide her away.

But the hole remained. She knew something had already passed through it.

As they approached the metal grate embedded in the middle of the road, Claire stopped.

To her, the grate seemed darker than the surrounding asphalt—like a wicked eye staring up from the earth. She turned toward Angelo, now just a silhouette against the fading light. Dusk had vanished, and night crept in with quiet finality.

"Before the complex was built," she asked softly, "what was here?"

Angelo hesitated. His eyes darted around the compound, as if searching for a way out of the question.

"If you want to know what's going on," Claire said, her voice low and steady, "you need to tell me the truth."

Unable to make out his expression, she watched as Angelo squatted beside the grate and buried his face in his hands. At that moment, the outdoor lights flickered on, casting an amber glow across the compound.

He stood slowly, exhaling a long breath of resignation.

"When they were laying the road," he began, "the engineer said we needed a drainage point here. Otherwise, rainwater would flood the units." He gestured toward the row of outdoor doors beside them. "So, I told him about the old well—filled in with rock. He said it was perfect. Already a hole. And filled with rock. So…" He shrugged, helpless.

Tom's face went pale. "You mean to tell us… this drain is the well where Sandra's body was buried?"

Angelo nodded.

Chaucer whimpered and backed away from the grate, tugging Claire with him.

No one spoke.

Claire turned and led them toward the far entrance of the indoor compound. Angelo punched in the code and held the door open. Just then, Claire caught movement near the grate—a small figure, outlined by the amber lights. A child, perhaps, racing across the open space toward the dumpster.

She said nothing.

She turned and stepped inside.

The rest of the tour passed in silence. No more shadows. No more visions.

Later, in the quiet of the studio apartment, they gathered around the table, eating and drinking in subdued reflection. No one spoke of the grate. Or the child. Or the well.

But all three knew something had been unearthed.

And it wasn't done with them yet.

"So, what's next, Einstein?" Angelo gruffed, scraping his plate and dropping it into the sink with a clatter.

Tom ran his fingers through his hair, irritated by the constant jabs. He looked away. "Oh, I don't know," he muttered.

Claire glanced at Angelo as he strolled back to the table. "His name is Tom," she said evenly. "Why do you keep calling him Einstein like it's some kind of insult?"

Angelo raised an eyebrow, unbothered.

Claire continued, her tone firm. "If it weren't for Tom bringing all this into the open, Sandra wouldn't have any help. She reached out to him—and he listened. You ignored it."

She pulled a collapsible bowl from her bag, poured in a pouch of food, and set it down for Chaucer, who lay quietly beside her chair.

Angelo harrumphed at the remark, stuck his unlit cigar between his teeth, and sat down. "Well, I don't mean anything by it," he said with a crooked grin. "It's just a nickname. That's all."

Tom had had enough. He stood abruptly; eyes locked on his manager. "Well, I don't like it."

Angelo frowned, surprised by the outburst. Claire remained quiet, pouring water into Chaucer's bowl after he had gobbled his food. The dog lapped it up eagerly.

"Hey, you're a college student studying science," Angelo said, trying to defend himself. "I meant it more as a compliment."

Tom's voice sharpened. "It's not a compliment. I'm not Einstein. And you *do* mean it as a put-down. You didn't go to college, so you feel the need to mock those who did."

Angelo was silent for a long moment. His expression hardened, then softened into something more thoughtful. He glanced at Claire, who kept her eyes on Chaucer.

He removed the cigar from his mouth, held up his hands in mock surrender. "Okay… okay. No reason to get bent out of shape. Your point's taken. We'll go on from here. No harm, no foul."

Tom hesitated, unsure if the apology was genuine, but slowly sat back down.

Claire cleared her throat, cutting through the tension. "As for what we do next," she said, "we wait. We're on *their* timetable, not ours."

She looked at both men. "I suggest we take turns staying awake tonight. One of us stays alert while the other two sleep. If anything happens… we'll be ready."

The room fell quiet again.

Outside, the cicadas sang louder, and the night deepened.

Chapter 9

Angelo took the first watch, beginning promptly at 10:00 p.m.

The evening had remained stiff between the three of them, their focus narrowed to the logistics of the night's vigil. There had been much debate. Angelo wanted to sit at his office desk and work while keeping watch, but Claire and Tom insisted he remain in the studio apartment—where everyone can be together.

After some grumbling, Angelo conceded. He brought in a small desk lamp and set up at the table, papers spread before him like armor. They agreed on a rotation: two and a half hours each. If anything occurred, the watcher would wake the others—no solo investigations. The only exception was checking the monitors in the office, and even that was to be done cautiously.

Tom gave up his bed for Claire, curling up on Angelo's cot with an extra blanket. When the time came, he'd return the cot to Angelo and take his shift. Claire would take the final watch, relinquishing the bed back to Tom.

With the lights off, save for the soft glow of the desk lamp, Tom and Claire fell asleep quickly.

The first hour passed uneventfully, which suited Angelo just fine.

But shortly after 11:00 p.m., the phone in his office began to ring.

Tom stirred slightly, mumbling something incoherent, but didn't wake. Claire remained motionless.

Angelo shook his head. *Fine set of ghostbusters,* he thought. *The ringing's enough to wake the dead.*

Irritated, he shoved his papers aside and made his way to the office. It was probably just a tenant calling late. No need to wake the others.

On the seventh ring, he picked up the receiver. "U Lock 'em Storage."

Silence.

He repeated the greeting.

Still nothing—except, perhaps, a faint whistling sound. Wind? Static? He couldn't be sure.

He remembered what Tom had said about the phone ringing all night, keeping him awake. With a grunt, Angelo slammed the receiver down, yanked the cord from the wall, and carried it back to the studio apartment.

That'll show the spooks, he thought. *Whoever they are.*

But as he set the cord down, the silence felt heavier.

And the night wasn't over yet.

Angelo had barely settled back at the table, the phone cord coiled like a dead snake on the tabletop, when the ringing started again.

From the office.

He stared at the cord, stunned. Slowly, he picked it up, turning it over in his hands. It was the same cord. The only cord. Still unplugged.

A chill crept up his spine.

He rose, heart pounding, and made his way back to the office. The phone sat on the desk, ringing steadily—its line still disconnected from the wall.

Adrenaline surged through him, tightening his chest. He scanned the room, eyes flicking to the monitors. Everything outside looked still. Normal. But the ringing continued, relentless.

He reached out, hand trembling, and lifted the receiver.

He didn't speak.

He just listened.

At first, there was only silence. Then, faintly—like a voice echoing from the end of a long, dark tunnel—he heard his name.

A plea for help.

The voice was soft. Feminine. Young.

His breath caught.

It was the same voice he'd heard the night before. The same haunting tone that had burrowed into his memory.

"Sandra?" he whispered. "Is that you? Where are you?"

No answer. Just the voice, repeating its plea. Desperate. Distant.

He couldn't take it.

With a cry, he slammed the receiver down—not in anger, but in fear. He backed away from the desk, wringing his hands as panic washed over him like cold rain.

He had to do something.

Anything.

Snatching his keys from the hook, he bolted through the reception area. He fumbled with the lock, threw open the door, and plunged into the darkness.

The night swallowed him whole.

The heavy metal door slammed shut behind Angelo with thunderous finality.

He froze.

The automatic lights didn't trip.

Darkness enfolded him.

He spun back toward the door, just a step away, and reached for the knob. Locked. His fingers fumbled for the keys, but in the blackness, they were indistinguishable. Panic surged. The keys slipped from his grasp and clattered to the concrete floor.

He dropped to his knees, sweeping the ground with frantic hands. Nothing. It was as if the keys had been kicked away—spirited off by something unseen.

Standing again, breath shallow, he peered over his shoulder. At the far end of the corridor, the faint glow of the door window offered a sliver of light. He banged on the door behind him, hoping Tom or Claire would hear.

No response.

The darkness pressed in, thick and suffocating. It felt alive.

He turned toward the distant glow and began to move. Halfway there, the A/C system shut down. The sudden silence fell like a curtain, heavy and absolute.

He quickened his pace.

As he passed the last intersecting aisle, something caught his eye—a figure, standing at the far end, bathed in a soft aura of light.

It was her.

The same shifting figure he'd seen before—child, girl, young woman. Now, she solidified into the young woman. Sandra.

Her voice echoed across the corridor, eerie and desperate. "Jerry. Help me, please!"

Angelo took a hesitant step forward.

Then, from the shadows, another figure emerged—tall, muscular, draped in ancient Native American garb. His face was painted green, streaked with black. A raven headdress crowned his head, its wings spread, its beak frozen in a silent scream like Claire described.

The sorcerer.

He wrapped his forearm around Sandra's throat. She screamed, clawing at his grip.

Angelo felt the evil radiating from the man, even from a distance. It was suffocating.

The sorcerer turned and grinned, eyes gleaming with malice.

Angelo stood frozen, helpless.

Then, a voice rang out across the complex. "Mr. Angelo, are you in here?"

The specter turned, distracted.

Sandra broke free and bolted toward Angelo, arms outstretched. He reached for her, heart pounding.

But the sorcerer didn't chase her. He turned into the shadows and called out—summoning something unseen.

Sandra reached him.

And just as she did, the lights flickered on. The A/C roared back to life.

Her form dissolved—evaporating into a fine mist that swept over Angelo and through him.

He gasped, eyes wide.

He could feel her.

Smell her.

She was real.

And she was still trapped.

Angelo was a different man now—perhaps a defeated one. Tom saw it clearly as he watched his boss sit motionless at the table, eyes fixed on nothing, body slack with exhaustion. He hadn't spoken since Tom found him standing like a statue at the far end of the storage aisle, frozen in place as though caught between two worlds.

Claire stood nearby, her expression sober as she sipped her tea. Chaucer lay unharnessed near the bed, relaxed but alert, his gaze flicking occasionally toward his master.

Tom turned his attention back to Angelo. "Mr. Angelo… are you okay?" he asked gently, placing a hand on his shoulder. "Can you tell us what happened in there?"

Angelo's head turned slowly toward the touch, as if registering it for the first time, then drifted back to its vacant stare.

"I've witnessed this reaction before," Claire said quietly, taking another sip. "It's a response to shock. Part of him wants to believe what he experienced. Part of him is still denying it."

She paused, watching Angelo. "Give him time. He'll come back."

Tom moved to the counter and poured himself a cup of tea. "I wonder why he went into the complex without waking us." He nodded toward Chaucer, who lay near the bed, eyelids fluttering with sleep. "If I hadn't heard him whimper and bark, I wouldn't have known Angelo was gone."

Claire took a seat at the table, her attention still on Angelo. She traced the rim of her cup with a finger. “Maybe we’ve bitten off more than we can chew,” she said softly.

Tom sat beside her. “What do you mean?”

She shrugged. “Just that maybe we’re dealing with something more than a ghost. Something older. Stronger. The sorcerer’s power might be beyond us. Maybe we should stop. Cut our losses. Let it go.”

Tom stared at her, stunned. “Are you serious? You think we should just give up? What about Sandra?”

Claire placed her cup on the table. “What about her? She’s dead. What does that have to do with us?”

Silence fell.

Tom stared at her; disbelief etched across his face.

Then, another voice broke the stillness.

“It has everything to do with us… especially me.”

They turned.

Angelo was looking at them now. His expression was calm, but his voice carried weight.

Claire smiled gently. “Welcome back to the real world, Mr. Angelo.”

Tom stood, energized by the shift in the room. “Can I get you anything, Mr. Angelo? Tea? Coffee?”

Chaucer rose too, stretching with a soft groan and wagging his tail, sensing the change in atmosphere—something had happened, something important.

Angelo nodded. “Coffee.”

As Tom moved to prepare it, he glanced at Claire. “You said that on purpose—to shake him out of it.”

Claire smiled but said nothing.

Tom returned with the coffee and placed it gently in front of Angelo, then sat down, his tone now serious. "Can you tell us what happened in there?"

Angelo crossed his arms, eyes glazing as he searched his memory. He spoke slowly, recounting the disconnected phone ringing in the office—Tom nodded, remembering his own experience. He described rushing into the complex, the door locking behind him, the lights failing to turn on, and the keys slipping from his hand. Later, they'd found them exactly where he said.

Then came the vision.

Sandra. The sorcerer. The moment the lights blared on and her essence swept through him.

Angelo shook his head in wonder. "As she passed through me, I could feel her. Smell her." He looked down at his hands, lifted them, and sniffed. A chuckle escaped him. "I can still smell her," he whispered, eyes wide with amazement.

He looked up at Claire and Tom, who sat quietly, listening.

"We need to do something," he said. "Sandra needs our help. And I can't do it alone."

Tom had only seen Angelo open up once before—when he first shared the story of Sandra and the hauntings. But this was different. Something had shifted. It was as if, when Sandra's essence passed through him, a part of her stayed behind and they had become one.

Claire reached out and took his hand gently. "I promise, we'll help you."

She turned to Tom. "But I wasn't kidding earlier. We're up against something far more powerful than a ghost. This sorcerer… he must've been the medicine man for that isolated tribe. But it was dark medicine. Evil."

She shook her head slowly. “I don’t know what kind of power he tapped into, but it was enough to get him banished. Enough to fracture the tribe. He must’ve discovered some incantation—something that summoned demons. Maybe even one specific demon. That could be the creature he controls in the shadows.”

She sighed deeply, the weight of it pressing down.

“If it weren’t for Sandra, I’d say we should walk away. That’s how serious this is.”

She paused, then gave a wry smile, trying to lift the mood just enough.

“So, buckle your seatbelts. It’s going to be a bumpy—if not dangerous—ride.”

“I think we should close it down,” Claire said after a long stretch of silence. She sipped her tea, her voice calm but firm. “Don’t allow anyone in. Isolate the facility until this is over.”

Angelo shot to his feet, stunned. “What? We can’t do that! I *can’t* do that!” His voice rose with urgency. “This is a business. I have customers. An owner I answer to. I can’t just shut it down on a whim.”

Claire set her cup gently on the table and turned to him, her eyes unfocused but unwavering. Tom remained quiet, watching the exchange.

“I can’t just shut customers out,” Angelo continued. “Some of them rely on this place for their livelihood. I don’t have the right.”

Claire chose her words carefully. “I imagine somewhere in the lease agreement, it gives you the authority to control operations as needed. For safety. For maintenance.”

She sighed. "I'm not suggesting a week-long shutdown. Just a day or two. Tomorrow's Sunday—a slow day, right?"

Angelo nodded reluctantly.

"Keep it open today," Claire said. "Let customers know the facility will be closed tomorrow for emergency repairs—plumbing, electrical, gas leak, whatever sounds plausible. Anyone else, you call and inform them. They'll come today if they need to."

Angelo rubbed his face, still uncertain. "I don't know…"

"If it helps," Claire added, "I have a friend at the police department. They might be able to provide some kind of official sanction if anyone pushes back."

Angelo looked down at his hand, remembering the moment Sandra's essence passed through him. He could still feel it.

He nodded slowly. "Okay. If it'll help Sandra… I'll do it."

They spent the rest of the early morning crafting a plausible explanation—a gas leak requiring immediate repair, with the potential for serious danger if ignored. Customers were told the leak was inside the facility, above ground, and that the gas had been shut off at the road as a precaution. Until the issue was resolved, the building would remain closed for everyone's safety.

Most of the regulars accepted the news with little more than a disappointed sigh.

But two did not.

Foster, who stored his lawn equipment in the unit near the dumpster, was the first to push back.

"I need access to my gear," he insisted.

Angelo pressed him. "Do you have lawns scheduled for Sunday?"

Foster hesitated, then grumbled, "No."

Angelo nodded. "We should be open by Monday."

"It *better* be," Foster snapped. "Or I'll take my business elsewhere."

He stormed out, slamming the door behind him.

Angelo turned to Tom, scowling. "I hope your friend knows what she's doing. If I lose customers over this, I'll be in trouble with the owner."

Tom held his ground. "She's not a personal friend, Mr. Angelo. I didn't invite her—she just showed up. And honestly, she seems to know more than we do about what's happening."

Angelo growled. "We only have her word."

Tom didn't flinch. Since confronting Angelo about the Einstein nickname, he'd found his voice. "You and I have seen enough to know she's telling the truth. You saw the witch doctor yourself."

Before Angelo could respond, the door burst open.

Stevens marched in, voice booming. "What's this I hear about you closing the facility?"

Angelo nodded calmly. "Yes, sir. But only until the repairs are completed and the site is considered safe."

"I'll decide what's safe for me and my property," Stevens snapped.

Angelo took a deep breath. "I'm sorry, Mr. Stevens. Your lease agreement gives me the right—and the duty—to close the facility when necessary. And this is necessary."

Stevens bristled. "I'll take this to the city council. If I'm locked out, I'll have your license revoked."

Just then, the door opened again.

A uniformed police officer stepped inside, followed by three plain-clothes detectives. Each wore a badge and a pistol on their belts.

The first of the plain-clothed officers was older, around fifty, with thinning gray hair and a mustache. He wore khaki trousers, a tan polo, and brown loafers.

The second was tall—well over six feet—black, muscular, dressed in a crisp white shirt, black trousers, and a colorful tie.

The third was younger, with short-cropped black hair, dark-tanned skin, and a notebook in hand.

The room fell silent.

Stevens turned, his bravado faltering.

Stevens narrowed his eyes at the older detective. "Is this the goon squad come to kick me out?"

The detective didn't flinch. "No, sir. We're here to ensure your safety—and everyone else's—until the gas leak is resolved."

"I don't need the police to take care of my safety," Stevens snapped.

The uniformed officer replied without missing a beat. "Then you'll have to convince the city and the public that police aren't needed for public safety. I think you'll find yourself in the minority on that point."

Stevens turned back to Angelo, gave him a steely glare, grunted, and stormed out without another word. The officer followed him out, heading to the patrol car parked at the entrance.

Just then, Claire stepped out of the studio apartment, smiling as she recognized the voice. "Mr. Angelo… Tom… may I introduce you to Detective Sergeant Lyles and his partner, Detective Corporal Washington."

"It's *Detective Sergeant Washington* now," Lyles corrected with a grin. "He passed his sergeant's exam and now hovers over me like a vulture, waiting for me to retire."

Washington chuckled. "Still waiting for the Smithsonian to return my call. I requested they take this ancient fossil off my hands."

Claire laughed aloud and stepped around the counter with Chaucer trotting beside her. Angelo and Tom remained where they were, watching the exchange unfold.

Claire extended her hand toward the two familiar voices. Each detective took it gently and then hugged her.

"I'll never say 'where are the police when you need them' again," she quipped.

Lyles turned to the third officer. "This is the newest member of our team—Detective Corporal Achak Waya. Just promoted. He's learning the ropes."

Waya stepped forward, his voice deep and resonant. "Nice to meet you."

Claire nodded. "By the way, how did you manage to convince the department we had a problem here?"

Lyles smiled. "Oh, you mean the *major gas leak*?" He passed a sly glance to the others, the kind that said everything without saying a word.

Claire glanced back at Tom and Angelo. "Yes, that's what I mean."

Lyles shrugged. "Like I told Stevens—we're here to ensure the safety of our community. You don't need to tell us more than that."

Angelo finally spoke, his voice tinged with disbelief. "You gotta be kidding me. You also believe this place is haunted? The police?"

Lyles looked toward the two men behind the counter. "No, we're not kidding. And if this woman says there's a problem with ghosts, you can bet on it. We've both experienced it firsthand," he said, gesturing to himself and Washington. Detective Waya stood slightly apart, his expression unreadable.

Lyles turned back to Claire. "So, tell me what's going on."

Chaucer padded ahead as Claire led the three detectives into the studio apartment. Over the next thirty minutes, she recounted everything that had happened. Lyles and Washington listened intently, occasionally exchanging glances. Waya took notes, his pen moving steadily—until Claire described the Native American medicine man and his appearance.

Waya paused, his brow furrowing. "Wait… are you certain it was a medicine man?"

Claire turned toward him. "Absolutely, Detective Waya."

He gestured with his pen. "But if you're blind, how can you describe his features so clearly? Are you even sure he was Native American, much less a medicine man?"

Claire's tone remained calm. "What you may not know is, I sometimes see more in the spirit world than I do in the physical one. Not always—but it happens. I don't know why. I think it depends on which side of the divide I encounter the spirit. If it's closer to our world, I see less. If it's deeper in theirs, I see more."

She reached down and scratched behind Chaucer's ears, thoughtful. "I'm still learning, too."

Lyles shifted in his seat and glanced at Waya. "Claire, Waya's ancestors are Native American. Cherokee, right?"

Waya nodded. "Yes. Both my parents were full-blooded Cherokee. My wife's Osage—but I don't hold that against her," he added with a faint smile.

Claire smiled back. "Then maybe your background can help us."

He shrugged. “Maybe. Maybe not. Most of us have assimilated. I don’t know much about the old ways. But my father might.”

He paused, then asked, “Are you sure it wasn’t someone dressed up like a medicine man?”

Claire shook her head. “No. This wasn’t a costume. He wasn’t pretending. He was more like a sorcerer or witch doctor than a traditional healer. And he radiated evil.”

Waya scoffed. “White people always think medicine men are evil because of how they look. I doubt he was.”

Tom finally spoke up. “Detective Waya, are your ancestors from this area?”

Waya nodded. “Close enough. Not this exact spot, but the general region.”

Tom leaned forward. “Have you ever heard of a tribe that set themselves apart? One that was shunned by the others—like yours?”

Waya paused, thinking. Then he shook his head. “Not that I’m aware of. But like I said, I don’t know much about the old customs or deeper history.”

Tom leaned forward. “Could you ask your father?”

Waya nodded. “Yeah, I can do that.”

Angelo, who had been quiet, found his voice. “How old is your father?”

Waya chuckled. “I’m the youngest of eight. He’s in his late eighties now. If there was a lost tribe in this area, he’d know. His father—my grandfather—lived to ninety-two. I’m sure he passed down a lot of history and tradition.”

Lyles gave Waya a nod, a silent cue.

Without a word, Waya turned and headed out, already pulling out his phone.

Chapter 10

The tiny community of Bright Wood sat thirty miles off the main highway, accessible only by a narrow dirt road riddled with potholes, eroded runnels near creek beds, and deep ruts that tested the suspension of even the hardiest vehicles. Its neglected condition was a fitting prelude to what Waya expected as the road emptied into the heart of the settlement.

Bright Wood—its name a cruel irony—was home to just over two hundred souls, most living in varying degrees of poverty. State housing dotted the landscape, a half-hearted attempt to alleviate hardship, but it did little to stir ambition among the residents. Those who left in search of better lives were often met with quiet resentment by those who stayed. Waya had been one of the few who left, carving out a modestly successful career in law enforcement. Yet among the remaining townsfolk, his departure was viewed with suspicion—envy cloaked in accusations of disloyalty to Native tradition.

As Waya's white sedan rolled through the rutted streets, faces turned. Frowns and furrowed brows followed him, eyes narrowed beneath weathered brows. The car came to a stop in a cloud of dust before an aging house with a sagging porch. The structure was unpainted, its tin roof rusted and patched. Aluminum foil covered the south-facing windows, and a weary window unit clung to the back frame like a forgotten relic.

Waya stepped out and scanned the familiar scene. Nothing had changed in the seven years since he'd left. Two old hounds dozed beneath the porch, a hand-pumped well stood off to the side, and garden tools leaned against a shed like weary travelers. The front yard was a patchwork of gravel and dirt, and beyond the house, a wire-fenced garden stretched toward the woods.

An old man sat in a rocker at the porch's north end, gently swaying, eyes fixed ahead as if watching something only he could see. He gave no sign he'd noticed the car.

Moments later, the front door creaked open and an older woman stepped out, wiping her hands on a faded apron. Her long dark hair was streaked with gray, and she wore a floral print dress that hung to her knees, paired with low-heeled shoes. She squinted into the sunlight, then broke into a smile.

"Land's sake," she cried. "It's my baby, come home for a visit!"

She turned to the old man, still rocking in silence. "See who's here? It's your son, Achak."

The old man nodded once, his gaze never shifting, his face serene and unreadable.

Inola hurried down the wooden steps and wrapped Waya in a warm embrace. Her name—*Black Fox*—had been given to her because of her hair, jet black from birth and unwaveringly dark through most of her life. Now, in her waning years, streaks of gray had begun to thread through it.

She was twenty years younger than Waya's father, Achak—the elder Achak—and his third wife. She had borne him two sons and a daughter.

"What brings you back here?" Inola asked, smiling. At sixty, her face was lined and weathered, but her warmth remained. Waya remembered her as radiant when he was a child. He used to brush her long hair each night with an antique brush passed down from his grandmother.

He returned her smile. "Always good to see you, *agitsi*." He reached up and gently rubbed her cheek. "How have you been?"

She shrugged and glanced toward the porch. "Oh, you know. The same as always. Hand to mouth."

A gravelly voice drifted from the rocker. "The real people have always lived hand to mouth. It is a blessing, not a curse."

They turned toward the old man, still rocking, eyes fixed ahead.

"Your hearing hasn't faded, *agidoda*," Waya called out.

The corners of the old man's lips lifted slightly. "A warrior's senses must always remain keen," he replied, his expression returning to its usual sternness.

Waya smiled at Inola, who rolled her eyes playfully. They walked arm in arm toward the house.

At the top of the steps, she said, "Well, we don't have a fatted calf to celebrate your return, but there's venison and greens enough for a decent meal. Are you staying?"

He nodded, and her face brightened. She slipped inside to prepare the food, while Waya remained with his father.

He pulled a stool close to the rocker, sitting beside the old man, who still hadn't turned to look at him.

"I'd like to ask you a few questions… about the old people," he said carefully, choosing his words with respect.

The old man nodded once, slow and deliberate. "Is this for the white law… or for your own knowledge?"

Waya sighed. "Both." He knew his father disapproved of his choice to become a lawman, a path that often stood at odds with tradition.

The old man hesitated, then nodded once, still gazing ahead at something unseen.

"Did Grandfather ever tell you about a nearby tribe that was shunned by the others?" Achak asked carefully.

Silence followed.

Achak waited. It was dishonorable to rush an elder deep in thought. Finally, the old man spoke.

"*Agiduda* told of the Tsalagi who lived close by. We were forbidden to speak to them. Forbidden to meet with them. They were different… cursed."

"Cursed?" Achak asked. "In what way?"

The old man shook his head once. "It was forbidden to speak of them. They are no more."

Achak shifted, choosing a different approach. He began to recount the events at the storage facility—the strange occurrences, the blind woman's visions, and the figure she described.

At the mention of the medicine man—*sorcerer*, as Claire had called him—the old man slowly turned his head toward Achak. The movement was deliberate, and Achak felt a chill at the sudden intensity in his father's gaze.

"*Kalona Ayeliski*," the old man whispered, eyes sharp and haunted.

Achak leaned forward. "*Kalona Ayeliski*? What is that?"

His father's voice trembled, barely above a whisper. "He is a Raven Mocker. One who steals from the dying. One who preys on their last breath."

Achak's pulse quickened. "And the creature he commands? The one that follows him?"

The old man's eyes never left his son. "It is an *Asgina*. A malevolent spirit. A demon, as the Christians would say."

Their conversation was cut short by Inola's call to dinner. Reluctant but respectful, Waya and his father rose and stepped into the small house.

It took a moment for Waya's eyes to adjust to the dim interior, lit only by a single oil lamp that flickered gently in the center of the table. The table stood off to one side of the living room. Across from it, nestled between two old but sturdy easy chairs, was a small end table with another lamp—unlit for now. Beside one of the chairs stood a modest bookshelf, its shelves filled with worn paperbacks and well-thumbed volumes that Inola kept close. Atop the shelf, a large Bible lay open at its center, as if consulted often and reverently.

A single door at the back of the room led into a tiny kitchen and an adjacent bedroom.

Waya paused, taking it all in. He had grown up here, back when the house was in better shape. Like many aging homes, repairs had slowed over time—not just from lack of money, but from the quiet exhaustion that settles over the elderly. Sometimes, it was simply that they could no longer see what needed fixing.

Still, Waya and his siblings had made do. As a child, he hadn't known any different. This was life in Bright Wood. And in some ways, they were better off than others.

By the time Waya was five, his older siblings had already moved out to start their own lives. He grew up with just one brother and one sister. His sister shared the back bedroom with their parents, while he and his brother slept on cots in the living room. To Waya, it had felt cozy—safe.

Back then, his father still hunted, bringing home venison and rabbit. His mother tended the garden, coaxing vegetables from the soil. In time, Waya and his brother learned to hunt in the old ways, and his sister helped their mother with the harvest. During certain seasons, their father taught them to use bows, passing down the skills of their ancestors.

Now, Achak was too old to hunt, too frail to care for himself or Inola. But as elders of the community, they were looked after by younger clan members. Inola, ever stubborn and proud, still insisted on tending her garden.

The table was set for three, and Waya took the seat he remembered as reserved for guests or extended family. A slab of baked venison rested on a platter near his mother, already divided into three generous portions. Bowls of black-eyed peas and collard greens sat within easy reach, and while everyone helped themselves, Inola served each plate a portion of the venison with practiced grace.

Once the plates were filled, Inola bowed her head and quietly offered a blessing. Waya lowered his head as well, though his eyes drifted toward his father, who stared ahead, unmoved. He knew his mother was a devout Christian, like many in the community, while his father remained steadfast in the old ways. Yet between them, there was never conflict—just quiet coexistence. Inola studied her Bible daily and attended church faithfully. When Waya was a child, she made sure he, his brother John, and sister Wilma went with her. Waya had grown up well-versed in Christian teachings and still held to them in his own way.

"So," Inola said, spearing a bite of venison, "what brings you to our neck of the woods?"

Waya nudged aside the collard greens and scooped up a few black-eyed peas, buying time to answer. His father remained silent, chewing slowly, eyes distant.

"Oh, you know," Waya said with a faint smile. "It was time to visit. And I needed to ask *agidoda* about some old traditions." He hoped to steer clear of anything spiritual.

But Inola was sharp—and quick.

"You think I don't have ears?" she said. "I heard you talking about *Asgina*. Is one of your investigations about demons? If it is, you'd better be careful."

Waya glanced at his father, who offered no help—still chewing, still silent.

"I know, Mother," he said gently. "Demons are evil. They come to steal, kill, and destroy." He echoed scripture, hoping to reassure her.

Her eyes locked onto his. "And don't forget Satan. He's the one who sends them."

Waya nodded respectfully. "Yes, ma'am. I know."

Inola glanced at her husband, then back to Waya. "You also mentioned a Raven Mocker."

He nodded.

She took another bite, chewed slowly, then said, "That's bad medicine. Be careful, my son."

The uniformed officer remained stationed at the gate throughout the day, directing arriving customers to the office. Inside, Tom manned the counter, steadily calling renters one by one, while Angelo explained the lockdown to each person who came through. Lyles and Washington lingered in the background, stepping in only when needed to reinforce the story. Most customers, upon hearing about the gas leak, left quickly. By late afternoon, the facility stood silent—emptied and abandoned.

The five of them gathered in the studio apartment as the sun dipped low.

"Terrell and I," Lyles began, "have a major operation tonight with the robbery unit." He checked his watch. "We'll need to leave shortly. The officer outside will rotate off, but I've arranged for another uniformed officer and his partner to take over. They'll stay on-site in case you need anything."

Everyone nodded as Lyles continued. "They'll park their cruiser inside the fence and set up in the reception area. Since they're on the night shift, they'll stay alert while you get some rest. If anything suspicious happens, they're under orders to wake you."

Tom asked, "Do they know what's really going on?"

Lyles shook his head. "Just the gas leak. So, I'd keep the ghost stories to yourself unless something major happens. If it does, they'll call us."

Claire leaned forward. "Will you come then?"

Lyles shrugged. "Depends on where we are in the sting. We'll respond if we're free."

He paused, then added, "Just remember—this isn't an official investigation. It's a safety operation. Like when patrol cars slow traffic after a big wreck. We're here to keep things calm, not chase shadows."

Again, they nodded, the weight of the evening settling in.

After Lyles and Washington departed, another patrol car rolled through the gate and parked near the office entrance. The officer stationed at the gate backed out and drove away without ceremony.

Moments later, two uniformed officers stepped into the office—one older, one younger. The senior of the pair, a slightly overweight man with a faded blue uniform and a gut that obscured the buckle of his Sam Browne belt, stepped forward. His hat sat crookedly on his head, and his expression was dry, humorless.

"Hello," he said, voice flat. "I'm Officer Scott. This is my partner, Officer Satterfield."

Tom immediately sensed that Scott viewed the assignment as tedious, something to endure rather than engage with. Satterfield, by contrast, stood a head shorter, her blond hair pulled back with a clip. Her uniform was crisp and newer, her posture alert. She held two large flashlights, while Scott carried a notebook. Her eyes flicked nervously between the group behind the counter and her partner.

Angelo, ever diplomatic, stepped forward. "Thank you, officers, for being here. We appreciate all the help the police can muster." He forced a smile.

Scott glanced around the room, unimpressed. "All the help we can muster? Doesn't look like you're being overrun by an unruly mob." His tone dripped with sarcasm. "We were told all leaseholders have been informed of the gas leak. Is that accurate?"

Angelo flushed, but Tom stepped in before the tension escalated. "Yes, sir. Everyone's been notified. What Mr. Angelo meant is that a few customers weren't thrilled about being locked out. Since we're a 24/7 facility, there's a chance someone might show up later and try to get in."

Scott nodded, seemingly satisfied. “Understood. We’ll set up here for the night and patrol the grounds every hour or two to make sure everything stays quiet.”

Claire spoke up. “Will you wake us if something happens?”

Scott squinted at her. “Do I know you, Miss? You look vaguely familiar.”

Claire shook her head. “Not that I’m aware of.”

Scott hesitated, thinking it over. “I don’t really see the reason for waking you. That’s why my partner and I are here—to resolve any occurrences.”

Angelo stepped in firmly. “I insist. This is our property, and we want to be informed if anything unusual happens.”

Scott paused again, his eyes narrowing. “Unusual? I assure you, we can handle anything unusual.” He glanced at each of them behind the counter. “Is there something you’re not telling me?”

They all shook their heads, exchanging quick glances.

After a moment, Scott shrugged. “Fine. If you insist. But I’ll warn you—don’t interfere with the performance of our duties.”

They nodded in unison.

Satisfied, Scott said, “Now that that’s settled, can you provide us with a couple of comfortable chairs for the night?”

Tom responded immediately, retrieving two chairs from Angelo’s office.

Once the chairs were in place, Scott said. “Now, who’s giving us the grand tour before it gets too dark?”

Angelo stepped forward without hesitation and led the officers out the door, leaving Tom and Claire alone.

Claire watched them go, then turned to Tom. “Do you think Mr. Angelo will tell them too much?”

Tom shook his head. "No. He wants as few people as possible knowing what's been going on. Honestly, I think he's hoping nothing happens at all."

Claire gave him a curious look. "I thought he was all in now?"

Tom considered his words. "Mr. Angelo's emotionally caught in the middle. It goes against his nature to believe in anything supernatural. But he's also haunted by what happened to Sandra—by the fact that he couldn't rescue her back then. This is his chance to make it right."

Claire nodded, her expression softening.

After a quiet moment, Tom asked, "Were you telling the truth when you said you'd never met Officer Scott before?"

Claire smiled faintly. "To be honest, I'm not really sure. I know he and his partner were involved in a case I worked on recently. I might've crossed paths with them at the beginning. I just… don't remember."

After Anola had finished cleaning the dinner dishes and spent a little time visiting, she quietly slipped into the bedroom, leaving Waya and his father alone in the dim living room. The lamp on the table had been extinguished, replaced by the faint glow of the smaller lamp between the chairs. Shadows clung to the corners of the room, stretching long and quiet as the moonless night settled over the village like a heavy blanket.

Though the house had electricity, Waya knew his parents used it sparingly—just enough to keep the refrigerator running in the kitchen. The rest was reserved for oil lamps and silence.

His father had remained mostly quiet throughout the evening, letting Anola do the talking. But as Waya unfolded his cot and began arranging his bedding, the old man finally spoke.

"The Raven Mocker will not be easily defeated," he murmured, his voice low and cryptic. "Especially not with the white man's guns." He gestured toward Waya's pistol and belt lying on the floor beside the cot.

Waya paused, then sat on the edge of the cot. "Why are you so sure? Because he's a spirit—not flesh and blood?"

His father considered the question, then nodded. "Yes. He is a spirit… an evil one. When he was alive, he ate the hearts of his victims." He let the words hang in the air. "It gave him immense power. Power he still uses."

Waya leaned forward. "So how do we stop him? We're not spirits. We're flesh and blood."

The old man nodded again, slowly. "According to what you've told me… there are moments when the land of flesh and blood overlaps the land of spirit. That is when he is most vulnerable."

Waya frowned. "Then why can't our guns kill him at that time, *Agidoda*?"

The old man shook his head. "He is protected from modern weapons. A gift granted by the *Asgina*."

A chill crept down Waya's spine. "So how do we stop him? He seems… invincible."

Without a word, his father rose and disappeared into the back bedroom. Moments later, he returned carrying an ancient bow and a quiver of arrows. Waya recognized it instantly—he hadn't seen it since he was a boy. It had been passed down through generations of their family. The quiver was made of deer hide, worn but intact. The bow, carved from the strong, flexible wood of an Osage tree, gleamed faintly in the lamplight. The arrows were rosewood; each tipped with razor-sharp obsidian.

The old man laid the set gently at Waya's feet, then eased back into his chair.

"This," he said, "is the only weapon that can pierce the Raven Mocker and destroy him."

Waya picked up one of the arrows, turning it in his hands. "But why this? Why not a bullet?"

"Because it comes from the time when the Raven Mocker still walked as a man," his father said, voice low. "It belongs to his world. And it will only work in that narrow moment—when flesh and blood overlap with the land of spirit."

After the lamp had been extinguished and the house settled into silence, Waya lay in the dark, his thoughts drifting between the words of his parents. His father spoke from the deep well of ancestral tradition, his mother, from the faith of her Christianity. Both carried a measure of weight.

As his eyes began to close, he heard a faint sound from the back of the house—a soft movement, deliberate and careful. A shadow emerged from the bedroom and crept quietly to his side. It paused, watching. Waya kept still, his eyes half-lidded. He knew it was his mother.

Anola bent gently and lifted the bow and quiver from the floor. Cradling them in her arms, she carried them to the Bible beside her chair, which lay open as always—its pages worn, its spine softened by years of prayer.

In the hush of the room, Waya heard her voice, low and steady. She prayed for protection over her son, her words tender and resolute. Then she blessed the weapon in her hands, invoking strength and safety.

When she finished, she returned the bow and arrows to their place beside the cot and slipped quietly back into the bedroom.

Waya smiled in the dark, a quiet contentment settling over him. Between the old ways and the new, he was covered.

Chapter 11

With the others off to bed and the lights dimmed, Officers Scott and Satterfield settled into their chairs in the darkened lobby. Outside, the moonless night pressed against the glass entrance, and the only illumination came from the pale vapor lights beyond the door. Inside, the soft hum of the A/C was the only sound.

Satterfield started to speak, but Scott raised a hand for silence. They sat in the semi-darkness for five minutes, letting the quiet settle over them like dust.

Satisfied the others were asleep, Scott crept to the studio door and gently closed it. He returned to his chair and leaned in. “I wanted to make sure they were out before we started talking.”

Satterfield whispered sharply, “You have no intention of waking them up, do you?”

Scott shook his head. “Nope. I see no reason to. We’re perfectly capable of handling trespassers without their help.”

She frowned. "I don't know… Mr. Angelo was pretty insistent. I don't want this coming back on us with the Sergeants."

Scott chuckled dryly. "Quit worrying about what other people think. You need to learn to handle situations on your own. Builds confidence." He let the words hang. Satterfield was still green—assigned to him earlier that year—and he was determined to pass down his brand of wisdom.

"Besides," he added, glancing at his watch, "I doubt anything's going to happen tonight. We'll do a sweep in about an hour." It was 11:00 p.m.

To cut off further debate, Scott stood and began pacing the perimeter of the lobby. Satterfield stayed seated, but he could feel her eyes tracking him.

He moved behind the counter and stepped into Angelo's office, sweeping his flashlight across the room. Everything sat in quiet hibernation—the desk, the filing cabinet, the worn chair, the clock ticking softly on the wall, and the monitors glowing faintly across from the desk.

He stepped around the desk and examined its surface: neatly stacked papers, a pen resting on a blotter, and a phone. He glanced at the monitors. The facility looked still. Too still.

Like a cemetery.

Just then, Scott caught a flicker of movement on one of the monitors—the one trained on the bend near the dumpster. It was so brief he couldn't be sure he'd seen anything at all. He squinted, watching for it to return. But the screens remained still, bathed in their quiet torpor.

Shrugging, he stepped out of the office and resumed his slow patrol around the lobby.

Another glance at his watch, surprised to see thirty minutes had passed.

At the door to the indoor facility, he paused and pressed his ear to the metal frame. The hum of the A/C was louder on the other side, but beneath it… something else. A faint knocking. Not mechanical. It moved—slowly—from one place to another, like footsteps muffled by distance.

He leaned away from the door and looked toward Satterfield, still seated, her eyes on him.

"Anything wrong?" she asked, her voice barely above a whisper.

He considered telling her, but shook his head instead and moved toward the glass lobby door.

Outside, the compound glowed under amber vapor lights. The trees beyond the units loomed above, their limbs reaching skyward like twisted priests summoning something ancient and dark. The sight unsettled him. He turned away before the night's spell could take hold.

His watch read 11:45.

"I think it's time for a tour of the facility," he said.

Satterfield nodded and stood, deferring to his lead.

Scott handed her the key to the indoor wing. "You take the inside. I'll walk the perimeter. You've got your radio—call if anything seems off."

She nodded again, flashlight in hand, and approached the metal door. He watched her open it slowly and step inside, the beam of her light swallowed by the dark corridor.

Then he turned toward the lobby door, the night waiting for him.

After Satterfield closed the door behind her, the lights of the first aisle flared to life—bright, sudden, and unsettling. The compound, once mundane, now felt uncanny, as if her patrol had slipped into something darker. The corridor ahead glowed like an eerie invitation, daring her to step forward.

Her adrenaline surged.

She took a deep breath and moved with deliberate precision, as though walking a tightrope. Her right hand hovered near the comforting grip of her pistol, while the flashlight in her left trembled just enough to make the batteries rattle inside the tube.

At the first exit door, she stopped. Her beam swept into the darkened cross-aisle to her right, then over to the exit door on her left. She stepped over and tested the knob. Locked. A slow breath escaped her lips.

Turning back toward the main aisle, she froze.

A shadow—faint, fleeting—slipped around the far corner of the cross-aisle. She squinted, raised her light, scanned the space. Nothing. Just rows of silent doors and the steady hum of the A/C, pulsing like a heartbeat through the walls.

Had she imagined it?

She waited, listening. The silence pressed in, broken only by the rhythmic thrum of machinery. Nothing moved.

She shook off the chill creeping up her spine and turned back to the main aisle. More doors to check. More shadows to face.

But before she took two steps, a sound echoed from the end of the same cross-aisle—the one where the shadow had vanished.

She was not alone.

Drawing a deep breath, she turned and stepped into the cross-aisle, leaving the comfort of the lights behind. Her flashlight beam cut through the dark like a blade.

Ten steps in, the lights of the facility blinked out.

The A/C fell silent.

Her flashlight dimmed… then died.

Darkness swallowed her whole.

The moment Scott stepped through the lobby door, a sudden gust of wind funneled through the compound, snatching his cap clean off his head. It lasted only seconds, but long enough to feel deliberate—like the facility itself was watching him.

He harrumphed, retrieved the cap, and tugged it back over the growing bald spot he preferred to keep hidden. Glancing to his right, he saw the glow of interior lights through the exit doors. *Satterfield must be making her rounds*, he thought.

Turning toward the gate, he sauntered to the ten-foot iron barrier, locked electronically to the fence. He jiggled it—secure. He sighed and looked up. The stars, brighter on the edge of town, stared down like a silent, angelic audience. He could almost hear their whispers. But down here, on his level, everything was quiet and still. Too still.

The silence was unnerving. Every breath, every shuffle of his shoes on the pavement felt amplified—yet swallowed instantly, as if the compound absorbed sound like a sponge.

He hated assignments like this. Playing security guard. Wasting manpower. He should be out chasing criminals, not rattling doorknobs and pacing concrete.

But here he was. Stuck.

He exhaled heavily and turned to resume his patrol.

Then he saw it.

A child—small, fast—riding a scooter at the far end of the entrance drive. Scott blinked in disbelief as the figure parked the scooter near the dumpster and darted around the corner of the building. Gone in a flash.

"Hey, you!" he shouted. "Stop!"

No response.

Scott jogged toward the spot, his gear clattering against his belt. He reached the corner and swept his flashlight across the area. Nothing. No movement. No sound. Just the same infernal silence.

He turned and walked to the dumpster. The scooter was still there—small, brightly colored, unmistakably a child's.

What child would be out here at this hour?

"And how did the kid get in?" he muttered aloud.

He turned, and his flashlight beam caught something behind him.

A gaping hole in the fence.

With a rising sense of unease, Scott stepped toward the hole in the fence, his flashlight beam slicing through the opening. But the darkness beyond swallowed the light whole. It was as if the void on the other side refused to be seen, a bottomless pit guarding its secrets.

He edged closer, careful not to lean in too far, sweeping the beam in a wider arc. Still, nothing. The light seemed to die just two feet past the fence—no mist, no fog, no obstruction. Just a wall of black.

"Impossible," he muttered.

He considered taking a closer look, but something—instinct, maybe—held him back.

Then, just as he turned away, a puff of cold air brushed his cheek. It made a sound—soft, deliberate—like an animal exhaling after catching a scent. He spun the beam back toward the hole, but it revealed only the same impenetrable void.

Shaking off the chill, he turned his attention back to the storage buildings.

That's when he saw it.

The lights inside flickered… then went out.

He froze. The facility's lights were motion-triggered. They should've responded to Satterfield's patrol. But no new lights came on. No movement. No sign of her.

His pulse quickened. Something wasn't right. Just then, the A/C compressors chugged to a stop.

He broke into a run toward the nearest exit door, adrenaline surging, the silence pressing in around him like a weight.

When the lights, flashlight, and A/C all cut off at once, Satterfield froze. The darkness around her became suffocating—so black and deep it felt almost solid, like a wall pressing in from every side. Her sense of direction vanished. The corridor she'd been walking moments ago now felt like a void.

Still, she was smart enough not to move. She kept her feet planted, holding her position as if tethered to reality. But even that felt futile.

She swung her dead flashlight in front of her, hoping for a flicker. Nothing. She slapped it against her palm, trying to jolt the batteries back to life. Still nothing.

Careful not to shift her footing, she glanced over her shoulder, hoping to catch a glimpse of light from the exit she'd checked earlier. But the blackness was complete.

Where am I? she thought. *Is this real?*

Her mind raced for options, but before she could act, a soft glow began to rise in front of her. It wasn't from the overhead lights. It had its own source—a pale lavender hue that shimmered at the end of the corridor. Slowly, the storage units on either side came into view, though their shapes and colors seemed warped, as if seen through water.

The glow began to take form.

A figure emerged—a young woman, draped in a lavender dress or shroud, her outline faint and translucent. Satterfield's eyes widened. She could see through her.

With trembling fingers, she reached for her pistol and drew it, keeping the barrel low.

"Who are you?" she called out. "What do you want? Identify yourself!"

The figure didn't respond.

They stared at each other for what felt like an eternity. Then, the ghostly woman began to move—gliding forward, her feet never touching the ground. Satterfield raised her weapon.

"Hold it right there! Stay back!"

But the figure kept coming. As she passed each storage unit, the doors rolled up and down in sequence, as if reacting to her presence. Satterfield swung her pistol left, then right, then back to the figure. Her voice caught in her throat. She wanted to shout—but fear held her silent.

Closer now, the young woman's mouth moved. She seemed to be calling out for help. Her arms reached forward, pleading.

Then, from the shadows behind her, something else emerged.

A monstrous figure shuffled forward. Its eyes glowed yellow and burning with menace. Its body was more solid than the girl's. It had the shape of a huge scorpion and stood as tall as a large dog. In the shadows, it stood upright on hind legs, pincers clicking with anticipation, studying Satterfield with cruel curiosity. It hissed and swung its massive tail over its back, poised to strike.

Satterfield screamed and fired three shots.

She heard the bullets thud into its armored-like chest—but the creature hardly flinched.

That's when she heard it: a distant pounding on a door, followed by the faint echo of Scott's voice shouting her name. But the sound was warped, as if carried through water—or from another dimension entirely.

The monster reared back, preparing to strike.

Satterfield's eyes darted to the ghostly woman. The specter turned, saw the creature behind her, and let out a scream—muffled and distorted, just like Scott's voice. Then, without warning, the young woman surged forward, her form flickering like a flame in the wind. Just as she reached Satterfield, she seemed to burst through an invisible barrier.

Her scream rang out clearly now, piercing the black void.

Satterfield caught her in her left arm, staggering under the sudden weight. "Stay with me!" she cried, holding the girl upright. With her right hand, she raised her pistol again, aiming at the beast. She knew the bullets were useless—but it was all she had.

In the shadows, the creature scuttled forward, its pincers snapping, its tail arched high.

Then—light.

The facility's overheads flared to life. The A/C roared back on.

And just like that, the darkness shattered.

Satterfield collapsed to the concrete floor in a heap, gasping. She sat up, blinking against the sudden brightness, her heart pounding in her chest.

The girl was gone.

So was the creature.

She slowly rose to her feet, disoriented, scanning the now-familiar corridor. Everything was back to normal—silent, sterile, still.

Then she saw them.

Mr. Angelo, his assistant, and the young blind woman with her dog guide were rushing toward her from the direction of the office, their faces etched with concern.

In the studio apartment, Satterfield sat at the table, still shaken from the ordeal, her hands wrapped around a steaming mug of black coffee. The others gathered around her—some standing, some seated—waiting for her to settle before asking questions.

Claire, the young blind woman, leaned forward and gently took Satterfield's hand. Her voice was calm, steady. "Are you ready to tell us what happened in there?"

Satterfield shook her head, her voice barely above a whisper. "I don't think I'll ever be calm again after what I saw."

"Just start from the beginning," Claire urged softly.

Satterfield glanced at her partner, seated beside her with arms crossed and face unreadable. Slowly, hesitantly, she began to recount her experience. At times, she faltered—embarrassed by how surreal it all sounded. But the others listened intently, never interrupting, never flinching. Only Scott furrowed his brow now and then, skepticism etched into his features.

When she finished, silence hung in the room like mist.

Claire broke it. "Officer Scott, did you encounter anything unusual during your rounds?"

Scott exhaled sharply, clearly annoyed. "Eerie, sure. But not unusual. I've seen strange things before."

Angelo leaned in, his tone edged with sarcasm. "So, what qualifies as eerie in your book?"

Scott shrugged. "No ghosts rattling chains, if that's what you're hoping for. Just a kid on a scooter. Real kid, I might add. I tried to catch him, but he vanished."

At the mention of the scooter, heads turned. Angelo gasped.

Scott scanned the room. "Any of you know this kid? Seen him before?"

No one answered.

He rose slowly from his seat, incredulous. "Wait a minute. You're telling me that what I saw out there… that kid… was a ghost?"

Still, no one spoke.

He looked from face to face, then to Satterfield, who remained silent and serious.

"You're not kidding?" he whispered.

Claire shook her head. "No, Officer Scott. We're not."

His disbelief hardened into anger. He jabbed a finger on the tabletop. "This whole thing—this hasn't been about a gas leak, has it?"

Angelo shook his head.

Scott's voice rose. "Then I want answers. I want the truth. Right now."

A voice rang out from the studio doorway. "The truth, Officer Scott, is what we're here to find out."

Everyone turned as Detectives Lyles and Washington stepped into the room.

"How the hell did you get through the gate?" Angelo asked, startled by their sudden appearance.

Lyles glanced at his partner. Washington answered, "It was open. We just drove in."

"That's impossible," Scott snapped. "I checked that gate myself. It was locked tight—I even rattled it. Solid as a rock."

Claire's voice cut in. "Why are you here? Is the sting operation over?"

The detectives moved closer to the group. "It ended over an hour ago," Lyles said. "Didn't you call us?"

They all exchanged confused looks and shook their heads.

Lyles raised an eyebrow. "Well, someone did. A call came into the station asking us to come immediately."

Blank stares met his words.

Tom finally spoke. "Someone might've called you—but it wasn't any of us."

The weight of that statement settled over the room.

Scott broke the silence. "Well, Satterfield and I are out of here. We've got real police work to do. Not chasing ghosts."

Lyles turned to him. "You're not going anywhere, Officer Scott. You and your partner are being temporarily reassigned—to my squad—until this is resolved."

Satterfield stood beside her partner, still unsteady but upright.

Scott bristled. "With all due respect, Sergeant, we've got better things to do than play ghost hunters."

Lyles stepped in front of him, blocking the door. "Your duty is to protect and serve the public," he said, gesturing to the others. "They are the public. And your second duty is to follow the orders of the officer in charge of this operation." He pointed to himself. "That's me."

Scott hesitated, jaw clenched. "Fine. Write me up. That's your call. But we're not staying. Find someone else to chase shadows."

He pushed past Lyles and Washington, Satterfield close behind. But when he reached the lobby entrance, he stopped cold.

The gate was closed.

He turned back to the group, now gathered behind him. "Okay… who locked the gate?"

No one answered.

"Never mind," he muttered, storming into Angelo's office. He jabbed the gate control button. Nothing. He pressed it again. Still nothing. He slammed it several more times in frustration.

The monitors showed no response.

He returned to the lobby, confused and fuming.

Claire's voice was calm but firm. "Looks like someone else wants you to stay too."

For the remainder of the night, they grouped into teams—Sergeant Washington, Officer Scott, and Tom took the outdoor patrol, while Sergeant Lyles, Officer Satterfield, Angelo, and Claire handled the interior rounds. Every hour, Claire and Angelo planned to alternate, keeping watch in the lobby. Chaucer, of course, never left Claire's side.

Outside, the compound greeted the team with a light breeze coursing through the compound, the rhythmic chirping of crickets from the forest beyond, and the occasional hum of a lone car passing on the distant road. But as soon as they turned to begin their rounds, everything stopped with abrupt suddenness.

The breeze died.

The crickets fell silent.

The isolation settled over them like an anvil.

Washington immediately drew his pistol, holding it low but ready. Tom followed close behind, eyes scanning. Scott, though, walked beside them, sighing, his pistol still holstered, his gait casual.

He doesn't get it, Tom thought. *But he will soon enough.*

As they reached the corner of the lot, Tom spotted the scooter—still leaning against the dumpster like a sleeping child. Washington paused at the bend in the drive, sweeping the area with his eyes. The night was utterly still. No wind. No sound. No movement.

He pointed at the scooter with his pistol, and Tom nodded. Scott shrugged, indifferent.

They turned to glance at the indoor structure, and that's when it happened.

A sudden rustling erupted beyond the wooden fence behind them.

Washington and Scott spun around, instinctively ducking. Scott's hand gripped his holster now, tense. Washington aimed his gun at the fence, tracking the sound.

Heavy movement crashed through the brush—limbs cracking, branches shoved aside, followed by a guttural grunt, like a beast charging its prey. Something scraped along the fence's wooden frame, then darted behind the dumpster toward the hole.

All eyes locked on the opening.

Tom's body trembled. He glanced at his companions—they were taut, alert, bracing.

Then, a pair of eyes appeared.

A malignant yellow. Menacing.

They hovered in the void of the hole, shifting from one face to the next, as if evaluating each of them. The unseen creature exhaled sharply, and a plume of breath rolled through the opening.

"Oh my God," Scott whispered, finally drawing his pistol. Tom noticed the barrel shaking in his grip.

The eyes stopped—locked onto Tom.

He felt it. Whatever it was… it knew him. Not just his face. His name.

"Let's slowly back away," Washington ordered.

No one argued. They retreated in unison, step by step, toward the center of the drive near the drainage grate. The creature scuttled away from the hole, back toward the woods. Then came the sound of frantic digging—claws tearing into earth. A muffled grunt echoed, and the compound fell silent once more.

"What in the hell was that?" Scott gasped, his breath ragged.

Washington shook his head. "I don't know. But I didn't like the look it gave us." He glanced at Tom.

Tom shook his head too. "It must be the thing Satterfield saw inside. I've heard it before… but I've never seen it. And it seems to know me."

The silence stretched.

Then, from beneath. Deep below the drainage grate, came a low, familiar growl.

Scott's face went pale. "Oh my God," he said. "It's stalking us."

Inside the complex, the lights remained extinguished, yet the A/C chugged along as if oblivious to the anomaly. The only light came from their flashlight beams.

"The sensors must be down," Angelo muttered. "I should check on that back in the office."

He turned to go, but Claire's voice stopped him.

"They're not down in the way you think, Mr. Angelo."

He paused, confusion flickering across his face. Then, as understanding dawned, his expression shifted—fear rising behind his eyes.

As a precaution, they agreed to stay together for the first round. Claire and Chaucer were essential for sensing any supernatural presence, and Angelo might be needed if Sandra reappeared.

"Can you see anything in this darkness with just flashlights?" Angelo whispered to Claire.

They all carried flashlights, including Claire, whose free hand remained tethered to Chaucer's harness.

"Not well," she murmured. "I can see the path at my feet, but everything else feels… empty. I'll have to rely on Chaucer more than usual."

Angelo nodded, then swept his beam around. "Why is it so dark in here? I can barely see a few steps ahead."

His light was swallowed by the gloom.

Satterfield, standing beside Lyles with her pistol drawn, said quietly, "I remember this. This is exactly how it felt when I was alone."

"This is a kind of divide," Claire explained. "Between the real world and the spirit world. We still feel the concrete beneath us, still hear the hum of the A/C—but the veil has thinned. The spirit world is overlapping ours."

She paused, then added, "And this one… is a world of deep darkness."

Satterfield's voice was tight. "You mean evil darkness? Because that's what I feel. Pure evil."

Claire nodded. "Yes."

Lyles, silent until now, spoke with quiet authority. "Stay close. No one drifts from the group."

They nodded and moved forward, the only sounds their footsteps on concrete and the steady hum of the A/C.

There now exuded an odious smell.

To Angelo, the walk down the first aisle felt endless. He saw no exit doors, no storage units—just the same oppressive blackness. It mirrored the night he'd first seen Sandra… and heard the beast above the wire mesh.

"I can't even tell where the intersecting aisle is," he said. "It's too dark."

They stopped and scanned in every direction, pairing their flashlights, hoping to pierce the gloom.

But the darkness devoured the light.

Outside, they peered down into the darkened drain—and saw them.

A pair of eyes. Menacing. Reflecting back at them from the depths.

Scott raised his pistol, ready to fire.

Washington grabbed his arm. "Don't!" he barked. "A bullet could ricochet off the metal and hit one of us." He exhaled slowly. "Besides… I doubt it would help. Might just make it angry. You heard what your partner said about shooting it."

Scott stared at him, wide-eyed. "So, what are we supposed to do? Just let it come at us?"

But before the words had fully left his mouth, the creature in the drain shifted its gaze—then turned away, vanishing into the shadows.

Silence followed.

Washington's eyes narrowed. "It's going after the others," he said. "Inside. Let's move!"

They sprinted to the nearest exit door and peered through the glass.

Nothing.

Just blackness.

"I thought you said the lights were motion-triggered," Washington said, turning to Tom.

"They are," Tom replied, his voice tight. "But I've seen this happen before."

All three began pounding on the door, shouting, hoping for a response.

Nothing.

Only the dark stared back.

Tom tried entering the code for the door several times, but the answer was the same, nothing…like the dark.

In the quiet darkness, Angelo heard Chaucer whimper.

He turned—and froze.

"Look!" he cried, pointing down the aisle.

They all turned at once.

A halo of lavender light shimmered into view, slowly forming a shape. First, a little girl. Then, a young woman. Once fully formed, she held her shape, though her body remained translucent. The glow reflected off the storage units lining the aisle. She was running toward them, her mouth open in a silent scream, her movements slowed as if caught in a dream.

"It's her!" Satterfield shouted. "The same girl I saw earlier!"

"Sandra!" Angelo called out.

The specter gained speed, her form growing clearer. Then, at the far end of the aisle, another figure emerged.

The witch doctor.

Just as Claire had described—tall, muscular, his face smeared with black and green streaks, eyes burning with fury. He turned toward the shadows behind him and pointed at Sandra.

From the darkness, a monstrous shape burst forth.

It moved in a slow motion, but its presence was overwhelming. The height of a great dane, it had the body of a scorpion—it's details still hidden in shadow.

Angelo opened his mouth to scream—but no sound came out.

Sandra's eyes flicked toward him as she ran, as if recognizing him. She was still screaming, but he couldn't hear it.

Then—*bang.*

A shot rang out.

Angelo turned. Lyles had fired at the sorcerer.

The bullet passed through the figure, clanging uselessly against the metal wall behind.

The sorcerer turned his gaze on them, eyes burning brighter. Then he laughed—silent and cruel.

Sandra and the creature accelerated, their forms blurring. In a flash, they blew past the group with the force of a sonic boom. Angelo, Lyles, Satterfield, and Claire were thrown to the floor as if struck by a blast wave.

The two figures spun through the facility in a blur of motion, forming a seamless vortex of light and shadow.

And then—*a burst of light.*

Gone.

Silence.

And from the exit door nearby—they heard the outside team break through the door.

Chapter 12

Back in the studio apartment, everyone sat or stood in dreaded silence, still shaken by what they had witnessed inside and outside the facility. The most stunned was Officer Scott, who sat numbly in his chair—his casual skepticism gone, his eyes fixed on his clasped hands atop the table.

Lyles broke the silence. "We don't need to ask Mr. Angelo whether it was Sandra we saw. And I assume the Native American figure was the sorcerer Claire described—and the creature, his familiar." He scanned the room for disagreement. Seeing none, he continued, "What we need now, if we're going to defend ourselves or fight back, is a clearer understanding of the spirit world we've been thrust into." He turned to Claire. "Claire, can you enlighten us?"

Claire glanced around, her eyes unable to fully read the expressions of those around her. She took a breath. "Every case I've worked has its own patterns—some familiar, some wildly different. I can sense parts of it, but much of it is still guesswork."

She leaned forward slightly. "First, we are definitely overlapping with a spirit world. And yes, it's an evil one. We need to let go of the Hollywood version of hauntings and ghosts. That's entertainment. What we're dealing with is real—in its own realm."

She let that settle.

"When we overlap into that world, it changes. Sometimes we're fully immersed, sometimes we're just observers. Time and substance behave differently there. Encounters feel strange because they don't follow the rules of our physical reality." She paused. "I wish I could explain it better."

She turned to Lyles. "Sergeant, you remember Jeff Barnes? He encountered the spirit of Cloe's abusive husband—both as a child and an adult. It was a force… and a person."

Lyles nodded solemnly.

Scott suddenly sat upright, recognition dawning. "Jeff Barnes! That's the guy who kept calling in break-ins. We responded to that. Satterfield, you remember?"

She nodded.

Scott pointed at Lyles and Washington. "You two were the detectives assigned to that case."

"That's right," Lyles confirmed. "At first, I thought it was a flesh-and-blood intruder. Until Terrell and I saw the finale ourselves."

Scott's smirk faded as the weight of Lyles's words sank in.

Claire continued before the moment slipped. "Whether you believe it or not, the ultimate orchestrator of this is Satan. That creature we saw—it was sent to control the sorcerer and destroy

Sandra. I believe it's been attached to him since his life on Earth. And it still is."

Scott crossed his arms. "Oh, bosh. You expect us to believe the Devil's behind this? What next—a priest flown in for an exorcism?"

Claire turned toward him. "Again, Officer, discard the media's version. This is real. Heaven and hell aren't entertainment—they're dimensions. The public's been fed a watered-down version."

Scott scoffed. "Evil exists, sure. But it's man-made. Man's inhumanity to man."

Claire's voice was calm. "And what about tonight? Can you explain what you saw?"

Scott stood and paced. "No. But I'm convinced there's someone behind this. A person. Pulling strings to make us think it's supernatural."

Claire quoted the book of Isaiah quietly, "'You see and recognize what is right but refuse to act upon it. You hear with your ears, but you don't really listen.'"

Scott looked around the room, caught in the weight of his own denial. But he quickly recovered. "We'll see what shakes out. My money's on a real perp." He glanced at Satterfield for support, but she looked away.

Claire turned back to the others. "For the rest of you—Satan, the demon, and the sorcerer are part of an earthly spiritual dimension. Not of heaven. But I believe God is watching. Guiding this to an end. That's why we're here."

Scott sighed loudly, but Claire pressed on. "I don't know why Sandra's trapped in this spirit world. Maybe because she died so young—before the age of accountability. Maybe this is more for our benefit than hers. Maybe she's a tool of grace, meant to open our eyes." She shrugged. "I'm still learning too."

Washington finally spoke. "That's all well and good, but it doesn't answer the real question—how do we fight this thing? You saw it yourself. Bullets don't work."

Claire nodded solemnly. "I know. Maybe your fellow detective, Waya, can shed some light when he returns."

The remainder of the night, they stayed away from the hot spots, camping out in the lobby and studio. The police officers and detectives dozed in the lobby and Angelo's office, while Tom, Angelo, Claire, and Chaucer took refuge in the studio apartment. Nothing further occurred after their discussion—to Lyles's relief—as though the spirit world had decided to grant them a reprieve.

As dawn broke, light pierced the glass of the lobby door. Scott and Satterfield stirred at the sound of a vehicle pulling to a stop outside. In Angelo's office, Lyles watched the monitor as the gate opened and closed on its own—no code, no button pressed. A white sedan rolled in. Waya's.

He raised his eyebrows at Washington, who stretched and rubbed his eyes, watching the screen. "And now the fun begins," Washington muttered.

Lyles chuckled softly. "You said it, partner."

They stepped into the lobby as Scott and Satterfield stood and adjusted their Sam Browne belts. Seconds later, Detective Achak Waya entered, trailed by two figures—an elderly man and a woman, older but younger than him. Like Waya, their faces bore the countenance of Native Americans, weathered yet dignified.

The man wore a brown long-sleeved shirt and faded trousers, his dusty boots clomping with each step. His hair was entirely gray, pulled back in a low braided ponytail. The woman's hair was black streaked with gray, double-braided, her blueprint dress and low-heeled pumps neat but practical. Both carried solemn expressions, though Lyles noticed a spark of amusement and excitement in the woman's eyes.

As the others from the studio joined, Waya introduced them. "Everyone, this is my father and mother—Achak and Anola Waya."

The elder Waya nodded, his face unreadable, carved in stone. Anola, however, stepped forward with warmth, shaking hands eagerly. "Pleased to meet you," she said brightly, before stepping back beside her husband.

Scott scoffed, unable to contain himself. "So, what is this? A powwow? Is this who you brought to rescue us from the evil we're facing, detective?"

Lyles's frown cut him short. "Keep your opinions to yourself, officer. Just do your job."

Scott bristled. "And just what is my job?"

Washington stepped forward, his voice firm. "Protect the public. Not insult them."

Scott shrank back, arms crossed, eyes on the floor.

Lyles turned to the Wayas. "I apologize for his outburst. We're all on edge, trying to understand what's happening and wondering what to do. Do you have any ideas how to help us?"

The elder Achak nodded, accepting the apology but remaining silent. Anola answered instead. "We will do what we can, Detective Lyles. Our son can explain."

All eyes turned to Detective Waya.

He drew a breath, glanced at his parents, and began. "According to my father, several generations ago, there was a small tribe in this area that followed the ways of an evil medicine man. He was considered *bad medicine* by all the tribes around them. He had a small following, but they eventually rebelled and left him. They mixed with other tribes and told stories of his practices—how he called upon the *Asgina* and *Uya*, malevolent spirits of the earth."

Waya's voice dropped lower. "The medicine man—really a sorcerer—was called a *Raven Mocker* by the elders. He wore a raven headdress and preyed on the souls of the dying. He tormented his victims until death, then ate their hearts to gain power. It is said an evil spirit did his bidding. The other tribes denounced him, forbidding anyone to enter his grounds or even speak his name."

At that, the elder Achak broke his silence. His voice was gravelly, yet firm. "When the white man came and took over the land, the place where the Raven Mocker lived was forgotten. Some say he never died but was taken bodily into the realm of dark spirits. Perhaps he died in exile, but no one knows. His spirit remains, bound to the *asgina* who protect him." He turned his gaze on Angelo. "Your ancestors must have settled on the very ground where he practiced. It is cursed."

Lyles leaned forward. "But how does the young girl fit into this?"

Achak's eyes narrowed. "Even in death, his spirit still preys on the souls of the dying, aided by his demon. The girl's death was sudden, untimely, and in his territory. She is caught between worlds. He wants her—but she resists."

Anola stepped forward, her voice clear and strong. "Let me explain in terms you may understand. My husband honors the old ways, but I am a woman of faith. Many in our tribe are. I respect the traditions, but I see them differently. This *asgina* is a demon, sent to control the sorcerer. He wants the girl's soul, but for reasons beyond us, she eludes him. And I believe God wants us to help her."

Her eyes fell on Claire. "Your blind girl is not here by accident."

Washington frowned. "What do you mean?"

Anola's gaze swept the room. "She is here for a reason. And so are we. To defeat the sorcerer and his demon. To free the girl."

"But how?" Lyles pressed. "Our weapons don't touch them."

Achak's voice was steady. "The medicine man lived in a time of different weapons. Guns will not harm him. He must be destroyed by a weapon he knows—one from his own time."

Washington's brow furrowed. "And what weapon is that?"

Detective Waya lifted a long canvas bag he had carried inside and handed it to his father. Achak opened it and drew out the ancient bow and a quiver of arrows. He pulled one arrow free and passed it to Washington. The shaft was long, its obsidian point razor-sharp, glinting in the morning light.

Scott scoffed again. "You've got to be kidding. How can a simple arrow kill something a 9mm can't?"

Achak turned to him, his gaze unflinching. "If I shot you with this bow, the shaft would slice through your body and out the other side. The Raven Mocker knows this weapon. He believes in its power. And belief is what binds him."

The police officers, detectives, Angelo, and Tom spent the day patrolling and planning, but the compound remained inert—lifeless, as though holding its breath. The light sensors obeyed their movements, the A/C hummed steadily, and outside, the scooter had vanished, leaving only the dumpster and the hole in the fence as mute witnesses to its presence.

In the lobby, the elder Waya sat alone, eyes fixed ahead or closed, as if preparing for a ritual.

Meanwhile, Anola accompanied Claire to the studio apartment. They shared tea in silence until Anola finally spoke. "Please don't be offended if I ask you something."

Claire shrugged lightly.

"Are you a medium of some sort? My faith doesn't abide mediums—or those who conjure the dead."

Claire smiled. "No. I'm not a medium. But I get that question often, so it doesn't offend me." She drew a breath. "My faith doesn't allow it either. I'm careful in what I say or do, and in how I try to understand these things. I conjure no spirits, and I don't speak to them. I have no spirit guide, nor do I tell fortunes. Most mediums, in my opinion, are charlatans—some with good intentions, perhaps—but charlatans nonetheless. They seek to perfect a skill. I don't. I take no money. My only purpose is to help and to understand."

Anola's eyes narrowed. "How do you know the devil—or some demon—isn't helping you?"

"That's fair," Claire admitted. "Honestly, I don't know for certain. But if I were controlled by the devil, the creatures we've faced wouldn't see me as a threat."

Anola nodded slowly.

"Perhaps I'm more like a prophet," Claire added softly. "Or something like it."

Anola set her cup down. "If you were a prophetess, you'd be speaking for God. And you'd know it."

"True," Claire agreed. "That's why I said, 'or something like it.' I don't want to project myself as a false prophet."

The older woman traced the rim of her cup. “I often wonder why we don’t have prophets today… like in ancient times.”

Claire pondered. “Maybe it’s like miracles. Perhaps we don’t have enough faith.”

Anola tilted her head, unconvinced.

Claire continued. “Like Officer Scott, we’re taught there’s a logical explanation for everything. That the supernatural doesn’t exist—only natural causes. Even people of faith struggle with that. It’s what we’ve been taught in our secular world. And we’ve traded real faith for superstition. Ghost stories on TV, books, entertainment. But this—” her eyes glazed as she gestured around them—“this is the real supernatural.”

Anola shifted the subject. “I notice you see, even though you are blind.”

Claire smiled faintly. “Blindness is relative. I’m legally blind. Some have no sight at all, but many, like me, see in degrees. I can distinguish shapes, like you sitting across from me, but not details unless I’m close. I can identify large objects if there’s enough light, because I’ve built a mental encyclopedia—trees, buildings, things I’ve learned to recognize. Basically, it’s all a blur. Some blurs darker, some with color. I can also detect movement fairly well.”

Anola chuckled. “In the old days, our tribe would have called you gifted.” Then her tone grew serious. “Why, then, can you see so much detail of the medicine man and his creature?”

Claire shrugged. “It’s a mystery I can’t explain.”

At that moment, the elder Waya stepped through the door. His presence filled the room. “Night approaches,” he said, his voice low and resolute. “And I am ready.”

They all gathered in the lobby just as the sun disappeared between distant clouds above the trees. Darkness pressed in earlier than usual, a heavy blanket of storm-gray, low-hanging clouds smothering the sky. It poured into the compound's interior like a leaden flood, swallowing the last traces of sunlight.

To Tom's dismay, the outdoor vapor lights failed to turn on. They hung lifeless, as though lulled into a psychic sleep. He pressed his face close to the glass door, but the gloom was absolute—he couldn't see six feet beyond the threshold.

Washington muttered, "That's not natural." His hand instinctively brushed the grip of his pistol.

Scott shifted uneasily, his skepticism eroded by the oppressive dark. "It's like the whole place is… dead."

Claire tightened her hold on Chaucer's harness. The dog's ears twitched, his body tense, sensing what the others could not.

The elder Waya rose from his chair, his movements deliberate, his eyes fixed on the blackness outside. "The night has come early," he said, voice low and resonant. "And it is not the night of this world."

Anola's gaze swept the group, her tone calm but urgent. "Stay together. The veil is thinning again."

The silence that followed was suffocating, broken only by the hum of the A/C and the faint shuffle of shoes on tile. Following Anola's advice, they stepped outside together. There, every shadow seemed to breathe, every corner of the compound waiting for something unseen to step forward.

Tom swallowed hard, his pulse quickening. *If the lights are gone,* he thought, *then we're already in their world.*

But the night wasn't finished. Conspiring with the enveloping darkness, a dense fog descended on the compound.

Now Tom could barely see Angelo beside him. Squinting to his left, he just made out Officer Satterfield, pistol already drawn.

The voice of Lyles carried through the fog. “Everyone, move in closer so we can see each other.”

Feet shuffled, and at arm’s distance Tom could finally make out the group—Angelo to his right, Claire behind him with Chaucer, the three Wayas clustered tightly together with their detective son’s gun drawn, Scott in front of Satterfield nervously clutching his firearm, and Lyles and Washington standing side by side, pistols lowered but ready.

“If you have a pistol drawn, hold your fire until I give the word,” Lyles ordered. “We don’t want to shoot each other.”

Washington’s voice was low. “Should we even be out here, partner?”

Lyles hesitated, then replied, “Being inside doesn’t mean we’ll face anything less challenging. We’ll take it as it comes.” He let that sink in, then added, “Let’s move forward as a group. Stay within viewing distance.”

As they advanced, Tom could just barely make out the frame of the facility to his right, beyond Angelo and the Wayas. The walk felt endless as they approached the corner where the drive bent and the dumpster sat. In the fog, time stood still. Flashlight beams failed to pierce the haze, bouncing back in dull reflection. It all seemed dreamlike, as though they had stepped into a netherworld without definition.

At the corner, they froze. The sound of squeaking wheels and tiny footfalls crossed in front of them, unseen, hidden by the fog. It stopped on the far side of the drive. Silence followed—then a metallic thump.

It’s the little girl on the scooter! Tom thought. *She must’ve dropped it by the dumpster.*

Angelo's voice confirmed his suspicion. "It's her… Sandra."

They listened, unmoving, for a long moment.

Then Tom's attention snapped forward. A grinding sound, followed by a beastly huff. A booming metallic reverberation pierced the night. A chill shot up his spine as a massive roar erupted, followed by rapid scurrying.

Like a blind man forced to rely on sound alone, Tom heard a girl scream—and a huge beast charging after her. They all stood powerless, listening as chaos unfolded. From the cacophony, it seemed the girl scrambled through the hole in the fence as her screaming muffled; then the creature crashed through after her, breaking branches and tearing through the forest.

It was heart-rending.

And then—silence.

"Everyone stay put," Lyles commanded. "Terrell and I will take a look."

"I'll go with you," Claire insisted.

"No way," Lyles countered. "It's safer for you to stay here."

Claire waved her arm in the fog. "And how will you find your way back in this? The mist is as thick as pea soup. I can barely see my own hand. I imagine it's just as bad—or worse—for you." She gestured toward Chaucer. "He can guide us back."

Lyles hesitated, then glanced at Washington. In the deep haze, Washington gave a low grunt of approval. "Okay. But stay close. Don't drift away."

Claire gave a soft laugh. "I should be telling you that. Chaucer and I won't have any trouble finding our way."

Lyles exhaled, reluctant but resigned. "All right then. Let's move. Stay close."

Claire ordered Chaucer forward. The dog seemed to know exactly where to go. Within half a minute, they reached the hulking dumpster. The scooter lay on its side, abandoned. Washington retrieved it and leaned it against the dumpster, just as he had found it earlier.

Claire watched as the detectives scanned the fog-drenched surroundings with caution. Chaucer waited, tense, then whimpered. Claire knew the sound well—it was his warning of a supernatural presence. He pressed against her right leg, trembling.

They moved toward the hole in the fence, which loomed before them like a menacing, dark eye. As Lyles approached, a low growl rumbled from beyond. He recoiled instantly, stumbling back.

"Watch it, partner," Washington warned, steadying him with one hand while keeping his pistol trained on the opening with the other.

Then, unexpectedly, Chaucer growled. Trained never to be aggressive, the threat was too much for him. He stepped in front of Claire, shielding her with his body. Claire stood only a few feet from the hole, beside Washington.

"I think we'd better back off," Lyles said.

Washington nodded. "Good idea."

As they retreated, the fog thickened, closing in like walls of smoke.

"Which way do we go?" Washington muttered. "It all looks the same."

Lyles shook his head, frustration edging his voice. He called out into the void: "Hey! Can anyone hear me? Shout out if you can so we can get a bearing!"

Only silence answered.

Washington looked around, his voice edged with panic. "They couldn't have been more than twenty or thirty feet from us! What happened to them?"

"This isn't a normal fog, detective," Claire explained calmly. "We've overlapped into another domain." She ordered Chaucer forward to find their companions, but Lyles raised a hand to stop her.

"It can't be that direction," he said firmly, pointing with his free hand while keeping his pistol steady in the other. "It's this way." Without waiting for confirmation, he started moving.

"Be careful, Detective Lyles," Claire warned. "Chaucer knows what he's doing."

Lyles didn't answer. He pressed ahead, convinced of his path. Washington and Claire followed silently with Chaucer straining against the harness, desperate to lead them the opposite way.

The fog thickened as they shuffled forward, swallowing them whole.

"Hey!" Lyles called out again. "Scott… Satterfield, speak up!" But only silence pressed back against his voice.

Then Claire froze. In front of them, with the haze partially thinning, shapes moved towards them—darkened forms, five of them, human in outline but wrong in their silence. Their footsteps were soundless, uncanny.

Washington's nerves snapped. "Hold it right there! Don't come any closer!" His pistol leveled at the nearest figure.

The forms ignored him, drifting closer, slowly encircling them with arms reaching.

"Hold your fire, Terrell," Lyles ordered, touching his partner's elbow. "It may be one of the others."

Washington's aim didn't waver. "If it's them, why are they walking like that? And why don't they say anything?"

Claire's stomach tightened. She remembered Angelo's words—that the back of the compound had once been a family cemetery.

Her voice cut through the fog. "We need to back out of here—quickly! They aren't our friends. Stay close behind me and let Chaucer lead us."

The two detectives obeyed quickly, unwilling to see what manner of beings was advancing on them. Chaucer moved with purpose through the fog, nose lifted, guiding them away from the monstrous forms. Before long, the mist began to thin, and they stumbled back upon their group.

"Where did you go?" Scott demanded.

"Sorry it took us so long," Lyles replied. "We got a little turned around coming back."

Scott harrumphed. "What do you mean *'so long'?* You were gone maybe fifteen seconds after you disappeared from sight."

Lyles and Washington exchanged uneasy glances as the others nodded in agreement with Scott's account.

Claire broke the silence. "I think we'd better head inside. We're not accomplishing anything out here."

No one argued. In wordless agreement, they turned toward the office entrance, trailing the outside wall with caution, each step deliberate as they guided themselves back through the fog.

Chapter 13

Back inside, at the elder Waya's suggestion, they gathered chairs from the apartment, office, and lobby, arranging them in a circle, within the open space of the lobby. "A circle is strong," he explained, "and cannot be broken by evil spirits."

They sat in silence, uncertain what to say or do.

"Well, here we are," Scott muttered at last, his sneer undercut by the tremor in his voice. "Finally in a Pow Wow." His bravado, though, had thinned considerably in the face of what they had just witnessed.

Claire turned toward him. "Do you still believe, Officer Scott, that a real person is behind all this? And if so, for what reason? If it's criminal intent, what would be the motive?"

Scott shrugged, his voice dropping to a murmur. "I don't know. But we need to keep an open mind about the possibility."

Claire's tone sharpened. "Seems the tables have turned. Now you're asking us to keep an open mind—not the other way around."

Scott crossed his arms in defiance, eyes shifting away.

After a moment, Lyles spoke. "Claire, you seem to have a better grasp of what's happening. Do you have any suggestions—or a plan—about how to proceed?"

All eyes turned to her. Claire drew a breath before answering. "I can only tell you what I perceive, and only what I know. In summary: Mr. Angelo's ancestors must've settled on the very ground where, generations ago, a small tribe lived under the rule of an evil medicine man. A sorcerer, really. His practices were so hideous, so steeped in dark spirits, that the surrounding tribes shunned him and refused even to speak his name. His small following eventually dissolved, leaving him alone in exile."

She hesitated, then continued. "I can't speak to the traditions of what became of him. But from my perspective, he died—yet was possibly raised again, in a counterfeit of what God did with Jesus. Raised not by holiness, but by a powerful demon."

Anola bowed her head and whispered, "Amen."

Claire smiled faintly at her, then pressed on. "Is this sorcerer truly dead or alive? I don't know. Perhaps something in between. He has become an evil servant, permitted to linger, continuing to practice his dark medicine."

"What is this evil medicine you keep talking about?" Washington asked.

"I assume," Claire replied, "it's the practices he once performed when he was alive—taking the souls of captives he sacrificed. And, tragically, a girl named Sandra was killed suddenly, perhaps near the very spot where he made those sacrifices. She died before her age of accountability, leaving her spirit vulnerable to capture. Since then, she has been fleeing her pursuer." She drew a short breath. "Though you may disagree, what I believe is that the true God wants her—and sent us to free her."

"Oh, for crying out loud!" Scott blurted. "How do you know that? I don't see God in this at all. If there's an all-powerful God, why didn't He just take her from the beginning?"

Claire turned her gaze on him. "So, you believe God is involved only if He does things your way?" She shook her head. "Man's attitude hasn't changed since the beginning."

The elder Waya broke in unexpectedly, his voice gravelly but firm. "The blind woman speaks the truth. The Raven Mocker captured souls for power when he was alive. Now he captures souls for the demon he serves in death. We must destroy him to break his power."

Anola added, her tone resolute, "And send him to hell where he belongs—and send this girl where she needs to be."

Scott scoffed, mocking again. "And where does Jesus fit in all this? I thought He was the Savior, not us."

Anola met his gaze with calm certainty. "He will. And we will know it when He does."

Scott fell silent, his skepticism unshaken, but his words spent.

Lyles leaned forward. "So how do we break his power?"

Claire hesitated, then admitted softly, "I don't know."

Scott, regaining his bravado, tapped the butt of his pistol. "With this."

Lyles shook his head. "I wish that were true, Scott. But I get the feeling it isn't."

Satterfield spoke firmly. "I know it isn't."

A heavy silence settled over the circle. Then the elder Waya's voice cut through, low and commanding. "We must confront him."

As the 1 o'clock hour struck, the group passed through the metal door into the ominous indoor storage area. This time Claire took the lead, Chaucer at her side. Lyles and Washington flanked her, pistols drawn, eyes scanning the shadows of hidden corners. Satterfield and Scott guarded the rear, while the others clustered tightly between.

Though tension ran high, nothing seemed amiss as they advanced. The automatic lights flickered obediently to life with each step across the sensors. The A/C drummed steadily, and the rows of storage doors stood like silent watchmen. The air remained calm—no cold spots, no sudden drafts, no chilling breezes to betray a presence.

Claire watched Chaucer closely as they turned each corner into new aisles. He neither whimpered nor shook, only panted lightly and licked his lips, a subtle sign of unease.

She herself felt nothing—only the blur of white storage units anchoring each side and the vague, unidentifiable forms beyond the reach of the lights. Compared to the chaos outside, it was almost anticlimactic.

When they completed the circuit and returned near the lobby door, silence hung heavy. Claire could almost sense relief radiating from the group as they stared at the inert surroundings.

"Well, that wasn't very profitable," Scott quipped. "Looks like our resident ghost has taken a powder."

The elder Waya's voice cut through. "No. He is still here… watching… measuring us." As the group turned toward him, he continued, "The Raven Mocker comes from the time of our ancestors. Silent, hidden, stalking. Even the white frontiersmen knew this."

Scott scoffed. "I didn't see or feel a thing." He glanced at Claire. "Did you or your pooch pick up any evil vibes?"

Claire shook her head but silently agreed with Detective Waya's elder father.

Scott's skepticism didn't rattle the elder Waya. His countenance remained impassive, certain.

Lyles broke his silence. "I suggest we head back to the lobby, take a break, and discuss our next move."

The group nodded in agreement.

As the others passed through the door one by one, Angelo caught Tom's elbow and held him back. He pressed a finger to his lips, demanding silence.

When the door shut, its metallic echo reverberating through the compound, Tom hissed, "Mr. Angelo, what are you doing?"

"You and I are staying behind," he replied firmly. "I'm tired of all this dilly-dallying. We need to act—fast. Every minute counts for Sandra." Seeing Tom's confusion, he added, "This isn't about them. This is about us." He paused for emphasis. "Sandra reached out to us. You and me."

Tom shook his head. "I'm not sure this is a good idea, Mr. Angelo. You heard what Claire and the others said. We're dealing with something more than just a ghost."

Angelo sighed in frustration. "Claire, Shmair! How do we know she's right? How do we know the Indian Chief is right? Scott's a hothead, and Satterfield's just a rookie. Listen—we can do this. Together. You and me."

Still hesitant, Tom muttered, "I don't know. We couldn't resolve it before. What makes you so sure we can now?"

"I just know," Angelo said flatly.

Tom exhaled in resignation. "So, what's the plan?"

Angelo rubbed his chin. "Step by step. Each time, Sandra seems to make closer contact with us. I think the answer lies in her."

Tom hesitated, then said, "That isn't much of a plan, Mr. Angelo."

Angelo shot him a look of consternation. "Just stick with me, Einstein. I know what I'm doing."

Before Tom could respond, Angelo strode down the main aisle toward the far end, forcing Tom to trail behind.

At the intersecting aisle in the corner, Angelo stopped. "This crossway… it's the one most affected. It's where Sandra's spirit passed through me."

They faced the yawning darkness together. Tom stayed silent until Angelo said, "Now we wait."

"Wait for what?" Tom asked.

Angelo's eyes narrowed. "Them."

Back inside the main area, everyone lingered for a time, soaking in the warmth of the lobby's security and the relief of the familiar. Eventually, though, they drifted back to their seats. Almost immediately, Lyles noticed the missing members.

"Where are Mr. Angelo and his assistant?" he asked.

Their chairs stood silent and vacant.

He glanced around. Each person shook their head.

"Did anyone see them follow us back inside?" he pressed.

Again, heads shook.

Satterfield spoke up. "They must've stayed in the storage area. But why would they do that?"

"Good question," Lyles said. He turned to Claire. "Any idea?"

"My guess," she replied, concern rising in her voice, "is that since they were the ones the spirits first contacted, they chose not to follow us—for reasons I can only guess."

Scott cut in, dismissive. "Well, they work here. I guess they can do what they want."

Ignoring him, Lyles built on Claire's thought. "Or maybe they were kept from following us—by the spirits—for their own purposes. In which case, we need to find them."

The group rose as one. Scott stood too, though reluctantly. "I say we wait. They might just be checking on mechanical issues with the compound."

Washington shot him a hard look. "What's the matter, Scott? Too scared to go back in?"

All eyes turned to him, waiting. Scott harrumphed. "Don't be ridiculous. I've faced worse dangers in my career than this." He pulled his pistol and strode to the door. "I'll even take point."

Lyles exchanged a smile with his partner.

Tom watched Angelo, as they sat waiting on the concrete floor, their backs to a storage unit door. He just stared into the darkness, waiting for a glimmer of lavender light. Tom marveled at his manager's certainty—this wasn't hope for what *might* happen, but certain hope in what *would.*

Occasionally, the sensors around them clicked off, plunging the area into shadow. Tom would simply wave his hand, and the lights flared back on. Angelo, however, remained still, content in both dark and light. When the lamps returned one time, Tom caught sight of a tear sliding down Angelo's cheek—something he had never seen before.

"You truly loved her, didn't you?" Tom asked softly.

The words pulled Angelo from his reverie. He turned, and Tom saw both cheeks stained with tears. "Yes," Angelo said simply. "And I still love her." He hesitated, leant his head back against the cool metal of the door and added, "When I lost her, that was when my train derailed." He thought back for a moment and said, "Even back then, I was unruly and full of myself. But she…she was gentle, obedient, and fun-loving." He shook his head. "Why she was interested in me, I can't figure."

He glanced at Tom. "That picture I showed you with her dressed in her Easter dress is precious to me, because it displayed her innocence and beauty." He laughed. "She tried so hard to get me to go to church with her, but at that time, I thought it was ridiculous and showed weakness. Instead, I pressed her to be more like me—unpredictable, wild, and defiant.

More tears began to fall as he unpacked the memory. Tom just listened. "It was my fault, you know, playing that hide and seek game outside the house. Sandra was hesitant to disobey our parents and go outside, but I persuaded her to be…spontaneous." He hung his head. "To me, spontaneous was just another word for defiant.

"I believe she was trying to impress me by doing something unpredictable and hiding in the well. But it backfired and I lost the one person I have ever loved."

There was a long pause in his story before he continued. During that moment the sensor lights went out, but this time, Angelo waved them back on with his hand.

"This whole compound," he explained, "is like a huge instrument. An instrument that I believe that was meant to provide me a way for a second chance. It brought me face to face with my fears, regrets, and, of course, my shortcomings." As he looked at Tom, Tom saw a look of peace cross his face. "I feel like…I've been forgiven." He sighed. "And now that I've found her—and I will never leave her again."

The finality of his tone puzzled Tom. He was about to ask what Angelo meant when movement flickered at the far end of the aisle.

At first it was only a spark of light, but it grew, taking shape, surrounded by a soft lavender aura. Tom's mouth fell open in astonishment. It was not the little girl on the scooter, nor the young woman he had glimpsed in the lobby, but an older, middle-aged woman—her features the same as her younger self—gliding forward in a flowing gown of radiant light.

"Jerry," the woman whispered. The sound of her voice seemed to brush Tom's cheeks like a gentle breeze.

They both stood, facing the apparition.

"Sandra," Angelo called back, his voice breaking with weeping.

Tom turned at the sound, his heart aching. When he looked back, Sandra had stopped halfway, as if held back by some unseen barrier. She lifted her arms, and before Tom could stop him, Angelo bolted forward. Tom took two steps to intercept, but knew it would be futile to try.

He watched in wonder as they met. Sandra embraced him, and Angelo too began to glow with the same lavender light. The union filled Tom with a strange, peaceful joy.

But as the reunion unfolded, another shape materialized at the far end. The Raven Mocker. Its face twisted into a look of triumph.

Chapter 14

As the Raven Mocker's gaze fell on Tom, his expression hardened, but no fear showed. Tom instinctively stepped back, uncertain, knowing the phantom was too powerful to confront in its own domain. After a brief pause, the Raven Mocker turned back to his quarry—now two instead of one.

He advanced with commanding confidence, intent on claiming his prize. Sandra glanced behind, saw him, and screamed. The sorcerer halted suddenly, his eyes shifting past Tom—over his shoulder.

Tom heard sudden movement behind him. Scott and Satterfield rushed forward, pistols raised. Without hesitation, Scott opened fire, his partner following suit. Gunfire thundered through the compound, echoing in Tom's ears. When their clips emptied, the Raven Mocker glanced down, brushed his chest with a hand, and laughed—mocking their futile attempt.

But his laughter faded into a frown as another figure stepped past Tom.

It was the elder Waya.

Like the Raven Mocker, he showed no fear. He strode forward, stopping a few paces away, his stance firm and expressionless before this ancient nemesis. The Raven Mocker regarded him with a quizzical look, then seemed to recognize him as a Native elder, though dressed in strange modern garb.

The two stood locked in silence. The rest of the group edged forward, aligning with Tom, waiting.

At last, the sorcerer spoke. His words were guttural, ancient, incomprehensible to Tom—harsh grunts and twisted syllables that sliced the air. He ended with a sharp hand gesture.

Waya nodded.

Tom turned to Anola, who watched in awe. "What did he say to your husband?" he whispered.

Without looking away, she answered softly, "I think he asked what tribe my husband was from, and why he chose to interfere. The gesture was a warning. My husband has kept up with our ancient dialects, though some have shifted over the years."

Then Waya spoke, his voice firm, his words cutting the air with equal weight. His hands remained still.

"He told him his time is over—that he must leave before he is destroyed," Anola explained.

The Raven Mocker digested the reply, then snorted in derision. Calmly, he raised his hand and gestured.

A roar tore through the darkness. From the shadows, an immense beast lumbered into the light.

"That's the monster I saw last night!" Satterfield shouted.

To Tom, the beast was even more hideous than she had described. It was a scorpion the size of a large dog, but larger than Chaucer and grotesquely human in part—its face was that of a man with long, tangled hair. Its eyes glowed, piercing and feline. A serpent's tongue flickered in and out between its lips, and when it roared, its mouth revealed fangs like a lion's.

It scuttled back and forth behind the Raven Mocker, restless, eager to strike. The sorcerer gave Waya a wicked grin and pointed toward Sandra and Angelo.

The monstrous scorpion reared on its hind legs, pincers clicking in anticipation, and let out a deafening roar. Then it lunged forward, tail arched over its head, venomous stinger poised to strike.

Tom's breath caught in horror as Angelo stepped between the beast and Sandra, shielding her with his body. The scorpion did not falter—it drove its stinger deep into Angelo's side.

At that moment, Tom heard Anola whisper, almost reverently, "The sacrifice."

"Oh my God!" Lyles shouted. He and Washington surged forward, pistols blazing.

The bullets could not kill the creature, but they pierced its armored hide, forcing it to stagger back. Its stinger tore free from Angelo's body, and Angelo collapsed to the ground, still clutching Sandra's flowing gown.

Claire stood off to the side of Tom, holding Chaucer as he whimpered in fear. As the intense drama unfolded, she saw with startling clarity the spirits behind the struggle. The Raven Mocker shouted a cry of victory—but his triumph was cut short when the younger Waya stepped forward from behind her, bow in hand, strung with a single arrow.

The elder Waya nodded, urging his son to take the shot. Instead, the younger man offered the weapon to his father.

The old Waya smiled at the honor. He took the bow, turned, and leveled it at the Raven Mocker. For the first time, the sorcerer's eyes betrayed fear. Yet when Waya pulled, the bow's powerful limbs resisted, bending only a few inches.

The Raven Mocker laughed, mocking his struggle.

Claire heard Anola's soft prayer: "Please, Lord, give him strength."

Then Waya grunted, straining, and—miraculously—the string drew back past his ear. The Raven Mocker's eyes widened once more in fear. In an instant, the arrow flew like lightning, burying itself deep in his chest.

The sorcerer stared in shock, unbelieving. He reached behind and found the shaft protruding from his back. He grasped it, tried to pull, but it would not move. For a long moment, nothing happened. Then his body began to shudder violently. He cried out in agony, his skin splitting apart, each half collapsing into oozing mush at his feet.

All that remained was a hideous skeleton, the arrow piercing its sternum. The bones clattered to the concrete floor, the grinning skull tumbling on top.

The monstrous scorpion, its grotesque human face twisted in outrage, turned toward the remains. It scuttled forward, seized the bones in its pincers, and dragged them into the waiting darkness. Claire could hear the anguished cries of the Raven Mocker's soul as it was carried off to its fate.

There was a moment's pause as Tom turned back toward Angelo and Sandra. Angelo still sat slumped against her, stung to the point of death. But just as swiftly as the Raven Mocker had been taken, a blinding light engulfed the entire complex. Tom shielded his eyes, and saw the others do the same. Seconds later, the brilliance faded, leaving them in the darkness of the storage area.

A moment passed, and then the overhead lights flickered on, as though nothing had happened.

"What just happened?" Satterfield asked.

Tom and the others turned. Claire stood with Chaucer at her side, over the very spot where Angelo and Sandra had been.

They were gone.

Scott, stunned, demanded, "Where did they go?"

"Not where the Raven Mocker was taken," Anola replied.

Scott pressed, "And where is that?"

Claire lifted her head slightly. "Do you smell that?"

The group fell silent, sniffing the air.

"Yes," Lyles said slowly. "It's familiar… rich." He looked at Claire. "What is it?"

"A sweet fragrance," she answered. "My guess would be nard, or something like it."

Confused, Lyles asked, "What is nard?"

Anola explained softly, "It's a costly, sacred oil used in anointing rituals. In the Bible, Mary used it to anoint the Lord's feet and head with her hair."

Scott scoffed. "So, you're saying Angelo and Sandra were anointed and taken to… Heaven?"

Claire shook her head. "You judge for yourself. But something wonderful has passed this way, leaving its fragrance behind."

Scott muttered in disbelief, but Satterfield's lips curved into a quiet smile.

As the group drifted toward the nearest exit, they stepped into the open air. The floodlights blazed across the outdoor complex, illuminating everything as though nothing unusual had ever occurred. Above them, the fog had lifted, hovering just beyond the reach of the lights, its edges shimmering into a halo of muted colors.

They turned toward the dumpster—and froze. The jagged hole in the fence was gone, sealed as if it had never existed.

Leaning quietly against the dumpster were two child scooters, placed side by side.

Epilogue

As morning broke and the fog lifted, storage owners lined up at the gate, eager to access their units. Tom opened the gate and left it wide. The crowd streamed in, no one questioning the lockout or pausing to complain. Business resumed as if nothing extraordinary had happened.

Scott and Satterfield departed without a word after Lyles formally released them. Waya drove his parents back home, telling Lyles he planned to take a few days off to spend with them. Lyles nodded with approval. "They deserve it. And so do you. Enjoy your visit—I'll clear it with the powers-that-be."

Later, Lyles, Washington, and Tom gathered in the studio apartment one last time. Claire sat quietly at the table, Chaucer at her side, her belongings packed and ready.

Lyles turned to Tom. "What will you do now, with your boss gone?"

Tom sighed, glancing around. "I'll finish out the day, settle everyone back in. I know how to run things now. At day's end, I'll call the owner, let him know Mr. Angelo didn't show up and isn't answering his phone. After that, it's his decision. Maybe I'll stay on through the summer—if the offer's right." He shrugged. "Why not?"

"Indeed, why not?" Lyles echoed with a smile.

He turned to Claire, who sat with a distant, taciturn look. "And you, Claire? Off to another case?"

She stirred from her reverie. "No. I think I'll take a break. I'm burned out after all this. Maybe a holiday somewhere—time to breathe."

Lyles frowned slightly. "Are you sure you're okay? You seem far away."

She met his gaze and smiled faintly. "I'm fine. Just tired."

He nodded, unconvinced. "Do you need a ride home?"

Claire shook her head. "I have someone picking me up."

"Who?" Lyles asked, curious.

A familiar voice answered from behind. "Me, that's who."

He turned to see Beth Wimberley at the door, stylish and prettier than he remembered.

"Hello again, Detective Lyles," she said, with a smile that made his heart skip. "Or should I call you Danny?"

Still stunned, he listened as she continued, "I'm here to collect on that dinner you promised me after the last case."

Washington clapped him on the back. "I think I can find my way home, partner. See you at the station."

As Claire rose, Beth's smile lingered. "Shall we go?"

Outside, the morning sun broke fully through the last veil of fog. The halo of colors dissolved into clear daylight, and for a fleeting moment, a soft fragrance lingered in the air—sweet and unmistakable. Chaucer lifted his nose, sniffing curiously at the scent, then padded forward and sat quietly, as if keeping watch.

Somewhere beyond the fence, unseen, a child's laughter echoed faintly and was gone.

The End

Acknowledgments

To my editor and publisher, Dr. Philip Levin, whose long hours of editing and excellent suggestions have fine-tuned this novel. Your knowledge and skills are greatly appreciated.

And, to my dedicated and patient wife, Becky, who provides me with the much-needed support and encouragement to write.

www.ingramcontent.com/pod-product-compliance
Lightning Source LLC
LaVergne TN
LVHW020046110826
845155LV00029B/640

* 9 7 8 1 9 4 2 1 8 1 6 0 6 *